Beneath Outstretched Arms

A Walk With Me Novel

VENESSA KNIZLEY

Beneath Outstretched Arms
By Venessa Knizley

Managing Editor: Loral Robben Pepoon, Cowriterpro
Associate Editor: Kayla Fioravanti, Selah Press
Prepared for Publication by: Kayla Fioravanti, Selah Press
Cover Design: Jennifer Smith, Eco-Office Gals
Cover Art & Illustrations: Amy Edwin
Psalm 27:13-14 Art: Alisa Taylor

Printed in the United States of America, Published by Selah Press, LLC
Copyright © 2016 Venessa Knizley

ISBN-13: 978-0692676387 (Selah Press)
ISBN-10: 0692676384

Scripture taken from the NEW AMERICAN STANDARD BIBLE®, Copyright© 1960, 1962, 1963, 1968, 1971, 1972, 1973, 1975, 1977, 1995 by The Lockman Foundation. Used by permission.

The definitions listed on the bottom of relevant pages and in the back of the book were compiled by the author from many online sources.

dedication

To my Heavenly Father, I love you.

Every good thing given and every perfect gift is from
above, coming down from the Father of lights, with
whom there is no variation or shifting shadow.
James 1:17

I would have despaired unless I had believed THAT I WOULD SEE THE Goodness of the LORD in the LAND of the Living WAIT for the LORD; be strong & let your Heart take courage; yes Wait for the LORD!

PSALM 27:13-14

©Alisa Taylor 2016
AlisaTaylorDesign.com

prologue

September 1348 Calais, France

The steady ebb and flow of the crashing waves joined together to form one all-consuming rhythmic, if not ominous, drone. The sound pulsed and swelled as it rose past the beach and rocky shore to encapsulate the man sitting high atop the cliff within its ongoing reverberations. Pensive, the twenty-three-year old knight dangled his legs over the edge, staring out into a bleak horizon. He tried squinting past the layers of dismal gray, but gained nothing for his efforts.

The sun was shrouded within a woolen blanket of clouds, and it became only too clear that what he was looking for could not be seen. *Lord, where are you in this?* His soul cried out. *What would you have me do?* Suddenly, the grass crunched behind him.

"Thought I'd find you out here," a familiar voice called out. "We could use you back in town."

Sir Makaias acknowledged his friend with a nod, but his blue eyes never wavered from their course. "Care to sit?" he finally asked, gesturing with his head to the spot beside him.

Sir Britton shifted his weight from one foot to the other as the salt sea air whistled passed his ears and wreaked havoc in his black hair. "Ah, no. The view from there is just a little too fantastic for me," he said, turning his attention skyward, already feeling uncomfortable with how close he was to the edge. Still, he craned his neck to take a peek.

i

"What are those things moving about down there on the beach?"

"Seagulls," Makaias stated flatly.

Britton let a shiver course down his spine. "They look more like ants to me. Are you quite sure you don't want to put some distance between you and the edge there?"

Undaunted, Makaias chuckled, his sandy brown hair dancing in the wind as he leaned forward to rest his forearms atop his thighs. "Do you know, on a clear day, you can see England from here," he said, extending his left arm out towards the horizon, before casually letting it fall back into his lap. "The white cliffs of Dover."

"Yes, I'm aware of that," Britton said with a smirk. "But is it really England you miss—or that little blond haired girl you talked into waiting for you back in London? We've served our time, you know. If Sir James sees fit to leave, we'll be going home soon enough."

Makaias shook his head. "I thought you'd already heard. He's staying—so we're staying."

Britton kicked at a stone in frustration.

"I don't know what we'd be going home to anyway," Makaias said, feeling weighted down by what he had to share.

"What do you mean?" Britton asked.

Makaias stood slowly to his feet, making one last effort to see his beloved England, before turning his face toward his friend and stepping back from the edge. His features were handsomely chiseled, yet rugged—his muscular physic befitting his occupation. "A ship came into port this morning. I spoke with one of the seaman—said he was from Bristol."

Side by side, the two men began the walk back towards the walls of Callais.

"That's a long way off. What's he doing here?"

"Apparently, he's made it his business to outrun the Plague."

Britton stopped to face him. "What are you saying?"

"It's reached London." Makaias said with feeling, letting the gravity of his words sink in.

"How bad is it?!"

"They're burying over forty men a day," he answered, running a hand over his face. "In some cases, sixty."

Britton was incredulous. "He couldn't have been serious!"

"There's no more room in the church yards," Makaias stated emphatically, "so they're digging mass graves—there are just too many bodies!"

"Is it that way everywhere—or just in London?"

Makaias shook his head. "I'm not sure, but he said when he left Bristol, it had already ravaged half the town—and that was only three months ago! The nobles have fled to their country estates to get away from the populous. They may fare better, but overall, everywhere he's gone…it's been the same."

"Bloody hell! So he decided to come here. The bastard's probably brought it with him!"

Makaias reached an arm across his chest to rub at his own shoulder, his muscles flexing beneath the heavy chain mail. "We already knew it was in Marseilles. It'll follow the trade routes—it's only a matter of time before it reaches us."

"This can't be real! What of our families?" Britton said, thinking specifically of his mother.

"It may be God's will to spare them," Makaias said, forcing a smile. "Look at us—we should have died in Crecy." Makaias placed a hand on Britton's shoulder and squeezed. "I don't know what God's doing in all of this. Perhaps…perhaps he's judging us for some lack of faith. But I know, for my part, that the only thing I can do is pray. We need to pray, Britton—to humble ourselves before Him."

"You always were more pious than I. Must be because of your mother's first occupation as a nun."

"Must be," Makaias said, trying not to let his mind wander into despair, as he thought about the desperate circumstances their families must be facing back in Totness.

"Let me tell you what I'm going to do," Britton said, interrupting his thoughts. "If we make it through this alive, I'm going to pray that you forget all about that little blond thing you're infatuated with, so that when we return home you can get to the business of marrying my sister."

Makaias chuckled, despite the morose nature that had just made up their conversation. *That little thing?* "I don't plan on marrying a girl, not yet old enough to put aside her dolls."

"Come off it, Velena's got to be…at least fifteen by now."

"You don't remember how old your own sister is!" Makaias laughed again. "Nor do you seem to recall that she's already betrothed."

"Pfft. Father doesn't want her to marry Peter. He's always liked you better."

"No offense, Britton," Makaias said with a smile, "but even if that were so, your sister's a bit silly for my taste—and Joanna's not an infatuation. What have you against her, anyway?"

"She's a merchant's daughter, for goodness sake!" And a *pretentious flirt*, he couldn't help thinking. "She's got no father, no fortune, and no future. Surely, you don't think that's the best you can do."

Before Makaias could answer, the clouds began letting down a light and even drizzle that drove them back to walking. *Lord help me.* "I've already given her my word, Britton."

"Don't let your chivalry get the better of you, Kai." Britton hesitated only a moment before adding, "And if London is in as dire straits as you say—you have to face the fact that she may not be there when we return."

For a moment Makaias just leaned his head back, letting the rain pad against his wind chapped face. "No offense, Brit—but neither may your sister."

"None taken—but I know my father! He'll have moved everyone to Wineford Castle. You said it yourself, they may have a chance if they can get away from the crowds. If things don't work out with your Joanna, consider the life you might have as a baron's son."

Makaias shook his head. He didn't want to think about

Britton's little sister. He wasn't even sure he could bear to think about Joanna right now. If he did, how on earth would he be able to carry on with his duties here, until he could get back to her? *Teach me to be faithful to your will, Lord, and not to my own.*

"I'd welcome you as a brother-in-law," Britton added.

Makaias smirked. "What? My friendship isn't good enough for you?"

Britton shrugged, as he gave his companion a hearty pat on the back. "A friendship can always be improved upon, can it not?"

December 1348, Landerhill Manor, Totnes, England

Velena ran a decent way from the gatehouse wall before finally stopping in an open field—no reason for stopping here, no reason at all. She felt alone, and that was enough. A rutted road wound on before her, leading towards a village green, and just beyond that to villeins'[1] homes. Many of which had become their inhabitant's tombs.

Though only fifteen, Velena's face wore a look of age, born from tragedy. Waist length dark brown hair hung loose down her back and around her shoulders. Her locks framed her face in a mass of waves and tangles, causing her green eyes to stand out that much more against fair skin that seemed to be growing ever paler.

The bleak December sky weighed heavily upon her soul as she closed her eyes tightly to the world around her. She rubbed her hands over her face. The ominous creaking of the windmill's giant rotating arms filled her ears as though there were no other sound to be heard. She stood in its looming shadow and trembled.

She was so quick to escape the confines of the house that she hadn't dressed for the cold, and the winter air pierced her lungs. Was it too much for her to hope that death could not touch her here, in the open air, or could this be where it waited—in the stillness, beneath outstretched arms that refused to stop and acknowledge death. Perhaps, this empty field is where she would take her first, last breath before her life ended.

Velena's heart thumped painfully within her chest; was it only

1

her imagination, or was it getting more difficult to breath? She looked back at the manor, clearly seeing its roof above the bailey walls, and the chimneys funneling down to neglected hearths within the manor, that should have been aglow with heat. The manor was a prison for all who lived there, suffocating and void of life, or at least of how life should be.

She didn't want to go back, but there was no going forward. Behind the manor, lay the acres of abandoned fiefs where the villeins had labored. No one worked anymore. They all just waited. They waited to live or waited to die—or to bury someone who did.

At least half of the people in the village were already dead—not to mention the animals. Pigs lay decaying beneath the forest canopy and dead sheep could be seen strewn across the fields, where they had been left to graze. The sheep were the first to go, and their remains left an awful stench that clung to the soil and permeated the air.

Creaking wheels suddenly caught Velena's attention. She turned towards the road. A short distance away, she could see two men, poorly dressed against the cold, emerging from the village—their faces indistinct. They maneuvered a two-wheeled cart over the ruts and bumps of the road until they veered off to the side, where a great length of ditch had been dug. There, they tossed the body of a woman into the shallow hole. Velena recoiled as if one of the lifeless limbs might span the distance to reach out and touch her. Eyes wide, she watched as they, with heads bowed, shoulders slumped, and hearts defeated, headed back to the wagon to gather the remains of yet another poor soul.

Velena's hands flew to her mouth as she saw them lift the body of a small child. *Oh God, what's happening?*

The ground was cold and hard, but still Velena fell to her knees, light headed, crying tears of anguish. *The world is ending! It must be so.* "Surely, your judgments are upon us now, Lord! Will there be no escape for us?" Pitiful cries escaped her mouth in great clouds of fleeting vapor, vanishing into the wind—along with any hopes she had of salvation. Would God answer her?

Surely not. No, if it was God who judged mankind, there would be no one to deliver them. It was now as it was in the days of Noah. God had promised never again to send a flood, but what about a plague?

A great cleansing was sweeping its way over the world—absolute in its ability to blot out life, and so for many nights, Velena had lain upon her bed in a cold sweat, half-panicked and unable to sleep. Was her soul right before God? When death came to swallow her whole, where would it take her? Heaven? Hell? Did it even matter? She was already living in Hell and she couldn't imagine Heaven anymore; the stench of life had hidden it from her.

Finally, spent, Velena lifted her head from the yards of amber skirt that had billowed out around her. Gathering its folds into her hands, she wiped her face dry of the tears that were beginning to crystallize upon her cheeks.

She rose to stand, taking one last look towards the hastily covered hole. She grimaced, knowing the grave was too shallow. It would only be a matter of time before the dogs would dig the bodies up, leaving the half-devoured corpses to rot on the side of the road.

She took a ragged breath and turned back towards home. If she was to die, she wanted to die alongside her family. She prayed that somehow, someone would bury them all beside each other in the churchyard, and not leave them vulnerable to all manner of beasts. As to the destiny of her soul, perhaps it was best left to God. Throughout her life, Velena remembered her mother saying that God was merciful—but she still didn't give much credence to that hope. After all, her mother didn't say that anymore.

[1] **Villeins:** A feudal tenant.

leaving

Velena's feet were dragging and her hands felt numb from cold when she heard her father's call from where he stood at the gate, still a good fifty paces away. He wasn't an overly tall man, but he was imposing nonetheless. Both broad and muscular, his physical presence commanded the respect and obedience of others.

Receiving no answer, he called again, galled by his only daughter's blatant disregard for his rules. Catching sight of her, he didn't wait, but instead walked toward her to close the distance between them. "I told you not to leave the manor under any circumstances! Was that not clear enough for you?!"

"It was."

"Then why did you disobey me?"

"I ...I—" Velena collapsed into tears once again.

She would have sunk to the ground were it not for the strength of her father's arms catching her into his tight embrace. He held her then, knowing nothing more needed to be said. He knew why. If he wasn't sidled with so many responsibilities, he would have been tempted to escape as well. But as it was, he shouldered the urgent and overwhelming burden of the well-being of his household, and he couldn't afford to despair.

Exerting minimal effort, Sir Richard Ambrose, the Baron of Landerhill, scooped Velena up into his arms. He cradled her as he had when she was but a child, carrying her past gatehouse and bailey, and on through the great double doors of Landerhill Manor.

"Velena, shhhhhh. Hush now; I understand. We all feel this way, don't we?" he said, laying a bearded cheek against the top of her head.

"Even you?" she mumbled.

"Especially me."

He set Velena down on her feet and motioned for her to precede him up the finely built wooden staircase leading to the private solars[2] on the second floor. Once he entered behind her, he bade her to sit upon the bed while he promptly gathered up a woolen blanket to wrap about the shoulders of his still shivering daughter.

"I don't know what to do with myself. I feel so numb," Velena said.

"Don't despair, girl; I've decided we're leaving," Lord Richard announced calmly. So if you want for an occupation, once you've warmed up, you can busy yourself with packing. One trunk only—we've not servants enough to handle all of our belongings. I'll be able to replenish our needs when all of this passes."

"You think it'll pass?" Velena said in disbelief, searching her father's face, and wanting so much to believe in hope.

"I dare not think much at all. Now is hardly the time to stand prideful before the Lord." Sir Richard crossed over to the window at the far end of the room, hoping to catch a glimpse of some progress being made below. Thoughtfully, he stroked his caramel colored beard, able to run his fingers through it now that it'd grown long and thick from lack of attention. "God numbers our days, Velena, and like it or not, we have no say in the matter. We can't choose how we die, so our only choice then is how to live—and we can't live here. It's depressing," he said, trying at a weak smile, "too much death."

Velena didn't laugh. "Where are we going?"

"North, to Wineford Castle. I've got the servants preparing for it now. I've sent word ahead for my bailiff, Rolland, to make ready for our arrival. If this Pestilence hasn't stolen all from us, we'll have isolation and food for a while still. Marriage to your cousin Peter will have to wait."

"Won't Uncle Magnus be upset?"

"It hardly matters."

"What if Peter doesn't want me later?" Velena looked as though she might cry again.

"First, it's not his decision. Second, though you be fifteen and of age, I wouldn't abandon you to marriage while the world burns down around us. He'll just have to wait!" He crossed back over to join Velena on her bed, taking her smaller hands into his larger ones. "This is hardly the time to send you off to begin a household of your own. And anyway..." he began, his blue eyes holding her tenderly, as his thoughts strayed to happier times. "I wouldn't be separated from you now."

"And Mother?"

"We're in agreement."

"Couldn't Peter and Uncle Magnus just come with us? And what of Cousin Stuart—and Rowan and Jaren? What hope do they have if they stay? Won't you encourage them to come?"

Richard's eyes rolled back in his head, "You'd do that to your poor old father? Haven't I enough to contend with?"

"How can you jest? Is there anything more important than this?"

"Although one could hardly expect me to escape immediate death here for a slow one there, I did, in fact, extend the invitation. Your mother would have hanged me if I hadn't done my all to offer her brother a safe haven. As for Squires Rowan and Jaren, as much as they'd rather pay homage to you—and who wouldn't—their fealty is to their lord and Sir John. They go where he goes, so that's that."

"He didn't accept?" Velena was incredulous. "I can't believe he didn't accept. Uncle Magnus chooses to stay behind?"

"Yes, and he'd no more part with his sons then I'd part with you."

Velena's chin quivered. "What if I said please?" she whimpered, trying to smile but only succeeding in looking all the more wounded.

Her father chuckled, "Worry not, Daughter. Your uncle is too ambitious to let his sons die. He has his own plans; and though they don't include Wineford Castle—they do include you—and my title. Rest assured, he'll wait for our return, and you'll be Peter's wife at the end of it all."

Velena looked doubtful, and though Sir Richard longed to soothe her, there was no time for coddling.

"Come now; all flesh is being tested." The Baron took his daughter's slim shoulders in his hands as he looked her square in the face. "Will you falter or will you stand? I can't make the decision for you."

"I'll do my best, Father."

"Good girl," he said, dropping a quick kiss atop her dark head. "Start packing then; I'll send Daisy in to help you. We leave in the morning." Another kiss and Lord Richard strode from the room, calling for Velena's lady's maid to come and assist her mistress.

Once alone, Velena's thoughts drifted toward Peter, her first cousin on her mother's side. He was five years her elder, blond-haired, blue-eyed, and terribly handsome. His father, who was her Uncle Magnus, had sent him away at the age of seven to start his life as a page, and though Velena had hardly seen him since, she held no qualms concerning their betrothal.

She'd practically grown up with his younger brother, Stuart, who instead of being sent away, had stayed at home for his training under Sir John, along with Squires Rowan and Jaren, who had been sent to Magnus' care for the same instruction. Rowan and Jaren were cousins to Stuart from two of his aunts on his mother's side. Velena adored her cousin, Stuart, having spent the majority of her childhood in his company. So in her estimation, despite knowing very little of Peter, if the elder brother proved to be anything like the younger, she supposed she ought to count herself very fortunate.

It was true that there was the absence of romantic love, but there was familial affection, commitment, and honor—a duty to one's family. Her worry was only that Peter would die before they returned to Landerhill. And then, God forbid, what if her parents died? She'd be alone. And being alone was worse than death. Would there be anyone left to walk this life with her then?

Listlessly, Velena looked towards her window; it was not yet midday. Despite the large amount of work that would surely keep them all occupied, she felt certain that this day would drag on. And its end would be no better than its beginning. Indeed, it was nights that she dreaded the most.

In better days, when Lord Richard planned his trips to Wineford Castle, the house and grounds would have been a beehive of activity. House servants would have chattered and bustled about, calling out orders to one another in preparation for their master's three-day trek north. But now, the house was anything but bustling. What servants remained, after death and desertion had taken its toll, moved through an emotional quagmire. They went from one task to another in slow mechanical motion, as though movement itself was not to be endured. Velena was no exception. Lost in thought, she was startled as Daisy slammed the trunk lid.

"All finished, my lady," Daisy said, matter-of-factly. Daisy, who was of similar age to Velena, was a distant relation on her father's side. She had been Velena lady's maid for the past two years. Daisy was a petite and curvy blond with uncontrollable dimples. At first, Velena had found her to be a bit clumsy and overly dramatic, but as of late, she'd found great comfort in calling her a friend.

"It's getting too dark to see well. Light a candle, Daisy." Velena looked around the ornately furnished room to make sure she wasn't leaving anything important behind.

She frowned as the dusky shadows of the day's end began to envelope the books still sitting on her small wooden desk. She wanted to take them all, but couldn't justify taking more than one as a necessity. Opening a cover at random, she squinted to read the words, but it was no use. Dusk had come without the blow of the horn—and why not? Death now came without the toll of bells. It was a sober truth. So many were dying every day that there was just no point in ringing the church bells anymore, unless, of course, they intended on sounding them all day and all night.

"Your bed's ready, my lady. Oh, but I must have packed your brush. I was hoping we'd beat the dark," Daisy said, standing before the closed trunk, attempting to lift the lid while holding the candle in in the one hand and rummaging around through the clothes with the other.

"Please, don't bother," Velena was quick to call out, imagining that, at any moment, they might have all the light they needed. "I don't care about my hair."

"You'll likely care about it in the morning when I have to brush out all those tangles."

"I won't complain. Here, bring the candle to me."

"As you like, my lady."

Velena accepted the flickering light from Daisy's hand and set it down by her beloved books, allowing the candle's eerie glow to encase the small stack before her. Forcing herself to come to a decision, she chose *Tristan and Isulte* as the one she would bring. She thought for a moment that she might do better to choose a happier story, but was unsure if it were even possible to evoke the kind of emotion it would take to enjoy such a book. Having decided to take the book, she let Daisy help unbutton her out of her clothes until both of them, bare and in their nightcaps, slid beneath blankets and furs. Velena was in her four-post bed and Daisy in the trundle below.

"Oh, nonsense—the candle." Daisy bit her lip. "Bitter cold and I leave it on the other side of the room."

"It'll go out on its own."

"Thank you, my lady. It's been intolerably miserable in here without the fires being lit, as they ought. I'll have to talk with Titus tomorrow about falling behind on his job. He'd better not forget to light the fires at the castle—or we'll all freeze for sure."

"Titus died this morning," Velena said flatly.

"Oh…I didn't know."

"It's alright. Too many to keep track of…"

"Do you think there's any hope, my lady? With us getting out of here I mean."

"To hope means you have to have faith in something—or someone, I suppose."

"Do you have faith?"

"I'm tired Daisy. Go to sleep."

"Yes, my lady—goodnight."

"Goodnight." Velena turned towards the wall, unwilling to close her eyes. *Go to sleep. If only I could.*

---

[2] **Solar:** A bedroom and living space.

delay

Still in the dead of night, Velena perceived that morning had come, and found herself walking through empty halls and down abandoned village roads, horrified that her father had left without her.

She finally happened upon a meadow where the grass had withered away, and was now marred by a large chasm surrounded by a ring of children. They were singing and dancing and tossing wild flowers that were continuously sprouting from their hair into the divide before them. Velena tried to ask them what they were doing and if they'd seen her father, but she had no voice. Less than a moment later, she was within the singing circle of children, peering over the edge of the chasm. In horror and disgust, she was greeted by the diseased bodies of the dead and the dying.

She retreated, but couldn't break through the ring of children. Oblivious to her struggle, they continued on with their insidious singing and dancing, and tossing in of their flowers—one for every soul lost, they seemed to say. Velena fought against them as the circle grew smaller, ushering her towards the precipice of the mass grave and certain death! "No!" Velena awoke with a start, panting and sweaty despite the cold. The candle had gone out and all was dark, but there came a whisper from the trundle below.

"My lady?"

"Daisy?" Tears began to flow freely from the corners of her eyes wetting hair and pillow alike.

"It's me."

"I'm sorry I woke you," Velena apologized, trying to still her breathing. "I'm alright."

"It's okay—I have them too." Daisy pulled her hand out from beneath the heavy bedding and reached up to place it atop Velena's blankets where her hand might be. "The sun will be up soon."

Responding in kind, Velena gripped the hand offered and turned on her side to look down into the inky blackness where Daisy lay. "I often wonder that it still bothers. Soon, there will be no one left for it to shine on. Have you thought of that? Only rocks and plants...and bugs." Velena smirked to herself.

"Perhaps it rises in defiance of death," Daisy whispered, "maybe it's on our side."

"I don't think so."

"Why not?"

"Because—God made the sun."

With one last squeeze, Velena retrieved her hand and both girls lay blind until morning, waiting for the *defiant* sun to rise. And it would, but winter clouds would block out the strength of its light, and for a time, night would rule in Velena's heart, despite the morning. She didn't know it yet, but the day would bring only delay, as her father would awaken to a feverish wife, who was lost in a delirium, spitting up blood.

At the first sign of Plague, her dear mother was quarantined to her solar with only their personal physician to attend her. It would mean death for them both. Lord Richard sat outside his wife's door on the floor amongst the scattered, unchanged rushes. Despondent, he ignored the chair and the food that his valet brought to him. He spoke to no one save God, trading back and forth between sitting and standing with his head leaned up against the door. He prayed not for Lady Cecilia's recovery, for he knew there was no hope of one, but only for a quick death.

Once the fever manifested itself, one could expect three days of vomiting up blood and insufferable pain. If death didn't come on the third day, there could be four more days spent in agony as the black buboes formed and oozed; the smell would be awful.

It was all awful, and these first few hours were no exception, as Lady Cecelia's groans and retching were almost more than her husband could bear. "I'm coming in, Cecilia! I won't let you die alone!"

Her voice passed through the door, weak and hoarse. "No Richard! Please...you must live."

"I don't want to live without you. I can't live without you; I can't..." A broken husband fell to his knees, unfeeling wood pressed against his forehead, his arms outstretched upon the door, "Cecilia. Cecilia!" He yelled, banging on the door with balled up fists, until the physician within begged him to stop.

"You'll give her no peace, my Lord. You must stop!"

Tears blurred his vision so much that Lord Richard could no longer make out the individual grains in the thick wooden barrier that stood unyielding between the Lady Ambrose and himself. "I'll stop," he choked. "But tell her I'm still here! I won't leave. I won't leave you Cecilia, do you hear?"

"She hears, my lord," came the sympathetic reply.

If it weren't for the plans he had for his daughter's safety and the unknown condition of his son, Britton, he'd have torn the hinges from the wall, gladly forfeiting his own life, to spend his last moments comforting his beloved wife.

Now cheerless and hollow, he lay motionless upon the floor—waiting. Velena wanted to comfort her father, but she had been mortified to see him pleading to be admitted into the very room where the dreaded disease now ravaged her mother. How could he be so quick to leave Velena behind? What if he too fell ill? She'd be alone! Her throat constricted painfully as she remained fixed, watching from the threshold of her solar. She was angry and bereft—and ashamed that she was too afraid to go to him.

On the second day, it happened that Lord Richard heard a

weak voice calling from within the room. Several valets, hesitant before to disturb their grieving master, now approached with caution. It was the dying doctor. Mercifully, Lady Cecilia's suffering had ceased, but the doctor was now too debilitated himself to unbolt the door, which he'd secured to keep the grieving husband out. The Baron stood still, collecting his thoughts.

"Shall we break it down, my lord?" came a voice at his shoulder.

"Yes," he said, followed by a quick, "...No!" He held up his hand and then ran it over his face in indecision. "I don't know. I need a moment to think."

Lord Richard paced back and forth, visibly distraught.

"I'll see to it," a confident voice spoke from the top of the stairs.

The Baron stopped mid stride. "Sir Tarek?"

"You've a trip to make, my lord. You ought to make it."

"It's not your responsibility, sir knight."

"I'm at your command." Tarek's scarred face was resolute.

Sir Richard hesitated. "She's to be buried at the church."

"Consider it done."

"And the doctor."

"On my honor."

"I'd owe you much, Sir Tarek. What would you have?"

"You're in need of a steward, my lord."

"Not any more. Landerhill is at your command. Geoffrey, fetch ink and paper; let's make this official."

the departure

The biting December air penetrated their fur lined cloaks as Velena huddled in beside Daisy on the open wagon, loaded high with luggage and supplies bound for their new destination. Sir Richard sat astride his horse, eyes focused on the two missing fingers of his right hand. He'd lost them eleven years ago at the Battle of Sluys, one of the first battles in a series of battles that would outlive him and his children.

He'd been a long bowman aboard one of the English cogs engaging the French fleet, 180 sales strong, anchored in the Zwin channel. The defensive attack was led by Admirals Quieret and Behuchet. They were not experienced seamen, and ignoring the better judgment of the Genoese Admiral Barbavera, they made the fatal mistake of chaining all their ships together in rows of three. They thought that the three ships together would stand as a solid blockade against King Edward's advance to Bruges. The chaining of ships had, in fact, only served to remove the sea crafts' maneuverability, allowing for a bloody land battle over the open water.

Several English cogs engaged at one time, as their archers raised their longbows and bombarded the French ships with a hail of arrows—twenty to every enemy crossbowman's two. The cog that Sir Richard occupied finally sailed in close enough to a French ship allowing their men-at-arms to climb aboard.

All too quickly, a young Sir Richard had found himself throwing down his bow in favor of his sword. Engaged in a heated skirmish, he was knocked off balance and relieved of his weapon.

Backed against the rail, his adversary's sword sliced through the air—Richard dodged left. His life had been spared, but not the two appendages from the hand he'd used to steady himself with. The first and second fingers of his right hand were there, and then they were gone—out to sea. That's where he felt like he was now, barely treading water and drifting aimlessly, minus a most precious appendage. Cecilia had been as much a part of him as his own arm or leg. She'd been his very heart, callously ripped from his chest.

He turned towards the wagon and saw Velena, young and beautiful, watching him with those sad green eyes of hers. He remembered cradling her only three days ago, soothing her pain and telling her that all would be well. Had she had time to cry for her mother?

Lord Richard cleared his throat and adjusted his position in his saddle; he was acting like a woman, weepy and weak. He was a man of battle! After he lost the use of his sword hand, had he surrendered to death? No! He'd rammed his shoulder into his attacker's gut, recovered his sword to his left hand, and cut down his enemy.

Off in the distance, the church bells rang out for sext. It was already midday and Landerhill's bailiff, Wolfgang Alder, circled around the wagon one last time, making sure all of the ropes were tight and secure.

"All is ready, my lord," he said approaching his master. He tried several times to gain his attention, but it was no use—Sir Richard was still out to sea—fighting for his life. The bailiff rested a frigid hand upon the Baron's wrist. "Lord Richard?"

"What?" he said, startled.

"All is ready."

"Very good," he muttered, unable to say more. Reaching down from his place on his horse, the two men gripped forearms.

"God be with you, my lord," Wolf said with feeling.

The Baron nodded, returning the sentiment. "Call Sir Tarek to me."

Wolfgang left his lord's side, motioning for the scarred knight to approach his master, which he promptly did.

"At your service, my lord."

Sir Richard kept his voice low. "As steward, you have the privilege of choosing your own bailiff, but you'd do well to keep Wolf on—he's a fine man. If he should fall victim to this wretched plague, choose your next man wisely. There's nothing worse than a deceitful man."

"I understand, my lord. Wolf is a good man, indeed."

"And so are you."

The younger knight stood taller, swelling under his lord's praise.

"Lead your men well, Sir Tarek. My absence may be lengthy, and I'll not have my home overrun."

"On my honor, I'll defend it to the death—even if I'm the only man left to do so." He unsheathed his sword, in order to lift the hilt up high towards his lord. "I pledge to you my fealty, on the cross of this sword and on our Lord Jesus Christ, and do promise to fulfill my oath of giving the Lady Ambrose and the good doctor a proper Christian burial, else may you return to find this blade resting beside my rotting corpse." He then leaned in to kiss the signet ring upon Sir Richard's hand.

"I know you will. I know you will..." Sir Richard placed his hand upon Sir Tarek's head, and so ended their goodbyes.

a reprieve

Now underway, Velena took note of what a solemn procession they made; all of them mourned the absence of their baroness, for she'd been sorely loved. They passed the water mill, forest, and her father's demesne[3] land before the wagon wheels rolled onto the cold and empty road that would lead them to Wineford Castle. The wagon was followed by an entourage of house servants, including a cook, personal valets, and several marshals in charge of the Baron's favorite hawks and hounds, which Lord Richard refused to leave behind, *to God knows who*.

Velena found herself wishing there was such a thing as a book marshal; maybe then she would have felt justified in bringing more than she had. Aside from Velena and Daisy, there were no other women in their sober party, and only one child, Sir Andret's eight-year-old page, Navarre, who rode behind the knight's squire, Roger Longfellow. He was one of fifteen squires in the company of knights. All men, save their driver, traveled on foot or horseback, various ones carrying packs or pushing two wheeled carts tethered with the dogs and a few goats.

Sir Richard's knights totaled ten in all, and except for two, they rode out in front with their own entourage of squires and packhorses, leaving a path in the snow now dusting the ground around them. Sir Andret and Sir John of Staybrook made up the rear guard. Sir Andret was of average height, handsome, and solidly built. He spoke only what sentences were absolutely necessary. Sir John of Staybrook spoke even less. Together, they said little, but saw much. They were an excellent guard.

Ten was a smaller number than the eighteen knights who Sir Richard had originally planned to ride out with only days before, but the Pestilence would have its parting gift.

The Baron took every precaution he knew of to keep them from sickness as they traveled. He and Velena, along with Daisy and Geoffrey, his tall and lanky personal valet, slept apart from everyone else. All others slept in groups of three. If one among them were to become feverish, the other two were to stay behind to bury him once he passed. They were to be left with an eight days' ration of grain for porridge, which would allow for one serving a day. If one or both of the two remaining survived, they were free to join the others at the castle after their eight days of self-quarantine were finished.

The reality of the matter was that, in two groups, more than one fell ill at a time, leaving only one man to do the job of tending and hacking out a grave in the frozen ground. And in both cases, quite unfortunately for the dying men, the servant still in good health, abandoned his comrades, leaving them to languish as soon as the wagon was out of site, setting his feet back towards Landerhill.

During their three days of travel, six fell ill leaving behind four groups and twelve men. It was a party of twenty-seven souls, who finally came into site of their destination. The hundred-year-old castle stood tall and solid—a bulwark against the outside world of disease and sickness—or so they all hoped. But much to the chagrin of the company of snow covered weary travelers, the Baron then ordered that they make camp in the nearby woods for eight days more before allowing them admission beyond the castle walls, forbidding them to associate with any villeins living in the small village to the east.

Frustrated but obedient, the men began to erect tents and strike bargains with God in hopes that the days ahead would prove that the Plague no longer slept among them.

Seven cold uneventful days came and went, the sun was setting and the men now drank their fill, toasting an uncelebrated Christmas and their last night in the forest. A modest distance away from the men, Velena lay beside Daisy in the crisp open air, choosing the warmth of the fire over the chill of their tent. Across the distance, she enjoyed watching them in their good humor, though she was, herself, sad to see it end.

The nighttime sounds and smells of the winter woods, along with the lack of sickness, had been wondrously healing for her. Despite the cold weather and crude conditions, she'd found sleep again—beautiful, dreamless sleep. It never came easily, but it always came.

Velena awoke the morning of the eighth day from such a sleep, feeling an unearthly calm hovering over her soul. She looked up from her place beside the smoking embers of last night's fire, hypnotized by the broken streams of light trickling through tangled treetops to reach the earth below. For the first time since leaving Landerhill, she felt the smallest glimmer of hope that they might live.

Velena lifted an arm skyward, letting a beam of light dance in between her fingers. Perhaps she still had a little faith after all. The darkness she'd carried began to lift, and tears, not yet cried for her mother, came with great abandon.

[3] **Demesne:** Land attached to a manor, and retained for the owner's own use.

wineford castle

"Hey Bowan, come back. I still want to play knights. Stop! Come on, please."

"Sorry Jonas, time for me to play knight for real. I've got to get over to Sir Fredrick for combat practice or he'll have my hide."

"Can I watch then? I promise not to bother you."

Bowan looked down at the five-year-old boy, who was all business trying to keep up with the older lad. He was the smithy's son, and there was no denying the resemblance. He had the same unmistakable look of his father: red hair, fair skin, and freckles to boot. He was a rambunctious and reckless boy, and add to that clumsy. Needless to say, he wore more bumps, bruises, and black eyes than anyone who Bowan had ever come into contact with, but he was no one to be laughed at. Jonas was as serious about becoming a knight as any young boy could be."

"You can come."

"Say, Bowan? Um, Bowan? How…how…um, Bowan?"

"I can't answer your question until you ask one."

"How old are you again, Bowan?"

"Nineteen."

"Say, I was counting and guess what?"

"What?" Bowan grinned, wondering just exactly where this was going.

"I'm going to be seven in two more birthdays, and also...and also in two more birthdays you'll be...you'll be, um...you'll be old enough to be a knight."

"And?"

"Well, that's good because you're...you're...my friend so you...can...can make me your page."

Bowan threw back his head and laughed, imagining what manner of trouble this poor child would be in if he was ever allowed near a real sword.

For a moment Jonas looked hurt. "Kat told me that smithy's sons don't get to be knights, but I told her that we were friends and that you'd let me be your page."

Bowan took the time to stop and look Jonas square in the face. He could tell the boy was in earnest and there was so much emotion behind those stormy gray eyes that Bowan knew that even one hurtful word might crush his little friend's heart. "I give you my word."

"Honest?"

"I'd never lie to you."

Jonas nearly burst out of his skin with excitement as he threw his thin arms around Bowan's muscular neck. "I knew you would—I knew it! I'm going to tell Kat!"

"I thought you wanted to watch me practice."

"I'll come back, but I have to tell Kat that she was wrong. And Bowan?"

"Get on with you then."

Forgoing what he'd wanted to say, Jonas smiles a big toothy smile and ran as fast as his little legs could carry him. He hadn't gone far before he stumbled and fell, adding yet another rip to his already torn hose, "I'm okay," he called back, completely undeterred.

Bowan winced and tried to picture the smithy's son running errands for him as his future page—God forbid they be anything of importance.

Eight-year-old Katrina stood in the doorway of her father's shop. She couldn't go in when he was working because that was the rule. *"Underfoot is no place for you to be when I'm working with my hammer. I have to pay attention to what I'm doing, and I can't be worrying about where you are."* This of course only applied to her. Her brother, Jonas, could go in and watch anytime he wanted to—except he didn't want to. In Kat's mind, that wasn't the least bit fair. She loved the smithy, all those sparks, and smoke. She loved the way the metal glowed just after coming out of the fire and how the water hissed whenever her papa plunged in a finely shaped piece of metal.

Whether a sword or a plate of armor, Kat thought her father was the most talented person she knew. Every knight in the castle depended upon him, and it made her proud.

"Kat! Kat! Where are you? Kat!"

Katrina frowned in annoyance of her little brother, "I'm right here…you don't have to yell."

"Guess what?"

"What?"

"No. Guess."

"I don't want to guess, just tell me."

"No, you have to guess."

"I don't want to. Just go away if you're not going to tell me!"

In the midst of their argument, a giant of a man appeared in the doorway dwarfing the two small children. "You're louder than my hammers. What are you two going on about?"

Kat's gangling arms crossed over her chest in the usual way. "Jonas says he wants me to guess, and I don't want to. If he wants to tell me something, he can just tell me."

The smithy frowned at his daughter, "A piece of advice, daughter: an obstinate look doesn't wear well on any woman—just remember that as you grow. And to you, young man, pick your battles. Now, apologize to each other."

Jonas was only too eager to make amends, for he still wanted to gloat over his news. Kat did the same, but not without a scowl on her face.

"Good, now tell us what you came to say, son."

"Kat you were wrong when you said I couldn't be a knight, because...do you know why?"

"Out with it Jonas." His father crossed his arms in such a way as made you wonder where his daughter must have picked it up in the first place.

"In two birthdays Bowan's going to be a knight, and he said that I could be his page because in two birthdays I'll be seven."

Owen raised a red eyebrow, "Jonas, what have I said about lying?"

"I'm not lying! He gave me his word of honor. It's true!"

Kat looked unsure, "Can a smithy's son really be a knight?"

"It's happened before," Owen said smiling, seeing no need to refute his son, and hoping Bowan would, indeed, be a man of his word.

"This is wonderful!" Kat leaped forward, grabbing her brother's shoulders with as much excitement as she had pent up angst only moments ago, "Do you know what this means, Jonas? If you become a knight, Father won't have any son to help him in the shop anymore, which means I'll have to do it! I've always wanted to be a smithy!" Her blond braid tossed about as she jumped up and down.

Owen threw up his meaty hands in surrender. "God help me. Your mother's is rolling over in her grave."

Jonas looked confused, "You said Mama was in Heaven."

"It's a figure of speech, Jonas," Kat stated, feeling very proud of herself for knowing.

"Well, wouldn't she be happy that I'll get to be a knight and Kat can help you with the shop?"

"She'd cry her eyes out! Now scoot!"

"Wait! Papa, who are they?" Kat pointed towards the gatehouse just as a wagon passed through to the inner curtain wall.

Owen rubbed his hands on his apron. "That, my wee one, is Sir

Richard Ambrose, Baron of Landerhill and Lord of Wineford Castle. I don't see the Baroness, but that looks to be his daughter, the Lady Velena."

Jonas stared up at his father in amazement, "You mean this Wineford Castle?"

"Aye, son. He's the lord of this castle and you must show him proper respect or you'll find yourself across my knee, or worse yet," he said menacingly, "locked up in the pillory.[4] Same goes for you, Kat." He laughed as his children's wide-eyed expressions.

"I'll be good," Kat assured him looking back towards the wagon. "Lady Velena must be the most beautiful lady I've ever seen."

"She's alright," Jonas said squinting his eyes.

Kat ignored him, "And look at the color of her tunic! I wish I could have one like that when I grow up."

"Now, Kitten, what would you be needing fancy colored tunics for in a smithy's shop?" he said, winking at Jonas.

Kat looked up adoringly at her father, "Good thing you reminded me. I was almost coveting."

"That's a sin, Kat!" Jonas was quick to accuse.

"I said, almost."

"Out of my sight! The both of you—and don't get underfoot!"

Quick as a wink, the two siblings ran off towards the stables, hoping to catch a glimpse of Bowan practicing with the quintain.[5]

---

[4] **Pillory:** A punishment device, fashioned with holes for securing both the head and the hands. Most often used as a means of public humiliation.

[5] **Quintain:** An object or dummy, mounted on the moveable cross bar of a post, used as a target for the lance.

the baron's arrival

Velena looked up as the wagon rolled over the moat bridge and under the hundred-year-old portcullis.[6] She sat in awe of the castle grounds, imagining how they would look come spring.

Once across the bridge and behind castle walls, Wineford boasted of an enormous outer courtyard, or bailey as it was more often referred to, containing both orchard and vineyard. Not to be outdone, it's expansive inner bailey held all of the usual accommodations: a stockyard, barns, granary, stables, and animal sheds, as well as several gardens and a fish pond.

The buildings themselves were rather plain and not much updated, but taken as a whole, along with the extensive surrounding woods, and the massive vine-covered keep that rose up from the north end, Velena had to admit that it was quite splendid—even in winter.

Not having been here since she was a child, she was relatively unfamiliar with Wineford, other than she knew it to be an older castle that, in some years past, her father had taken some pains to have altered for comfort's sake. As they neared the inner bailey, Velena felt lost in the clamor of activity as servants and valets swarmed about them, emptying the wagon and carts, so that others could stable the horses and kennel the dogs.

Then there came Wineford's bailiff, Sir Rolland, to welcome the long absent Baron back to his home away from home. Unlike Wolfgang at Landerhill, who was an appointed vassal, Sir Rolland rented the castle and its lands from Sir Richard. Sir Rolland ran it as a lord in Sir Richard's stead.

Velena looked at the bailiff with curiosity. He appeared to be an older man, perhaps in his late forties. He had mousy brown hair, a mustache, and at least a weeks' worth of beard growth. He wasn't overly handsome, but he had the most amazing brown eyes that were just...well, wonderful. There was no other word to describe them. Not only were his eyes physically attractive, but they emanated kindness, if such a thing were possible.

Velena took a deep breath and smiled, immediately feeling at ease in his presence. She tore her gaze away from her father's man, and once again looked about. *So this is home,* she thought. *For how long?*

Velena scanned the crowd of faces surrounding her. She had grown comfortable with her traveling companions over the last week; no one had grown sick or died, and she'd been at peace—or at least her version of it. But here were new people, and in her mind that meant new danger of the Pestilence. She prayed with all her heart that she'd not moved from one graveyard to another.

---

[6] **Portcullis:** A heavy latticed grille, vertically-closing gate.

a warm welcome

Lord Rolland approached the Baron, embraced him, and then kissed his ring. "It does my heart good to see you well, my Lord Richard; may God continue to keep you in such a condition. Though these are dark times, indeed, I choose only to acknowledge that it is the outstretched arm of providence that has driven you back to us—and for that, we're grateful; for your presence is dearly loved by all."

"One might wonder how I could have stayed away so long with sentiments such as these waiting to greet me. Thank you for your kind words, Lord Rolland. It is, indeed, a great relief for us to be here."

"And the Baroness?"

Sir Richard shook his head, emotion threatening to resurface. "Let's go inside; we've come to you cold and weary of heart; there will be plenty of time for talk."

"Yes, of course, come in; all has been made ready for you."

Sir Richard's knights held back, opting instead to first see to their own horses and gear. The knights were wanting to look over the suitability of the stables and the barracks, in which they would sleep. The squires and the single page, Navarre, followed suit, stalked some distance away by an overwhelmingly pleased Jonas. Sir Richard and the rest of his household succeeded Lord Rolland into the great hall.

The hall, once existing as the first floor of the keep, now endured as a separate long, rectangular stone building standing perpendicular to the east inner curtain wall. It was large and spacious, and surprisingly bright because of eight glass-pained windows that lined the two longest walls; four on one side and four on the other, each with a pair of wooden shutters that could be secured, if need be.

Each row of windows was interrupted midway by a roughhewn stone fireplace, decorated with an ornately-carved wooden mantelpiece and a beautifully woven tapestry hanging immediately above it. The stone walls of the great hall were plastered over and painted from floor to ceiling with murals of flowers and scenes from King Arthur's court.

The exposed beams of the vaulted ceiling only added to the airy beauty of the room. Freshly spread rushes and sweet smelling herbs blanketed the hard wood floors leading up to the wooden dais,[7] a platform on which a permanent table was set up for use by the lord's family and honored guests.

Other than the dais and the beautifully engraved chairs that accompanied it, the only other furnishings were a plethora of wooden tables and benches, some of which lined the walls to be set out during meals. Several had been set up in front of the lit fireplaces for casual visiting and the drinking of hot-spiced wine.

Velena, who was now seated next to her father at the head table, exchanged an amused look with Daisy, who was seated at one of the lower tables with the other valets and Wineford Castle servants, who were also filtering in.

Daisy was being ogled from across the hall by Sir Fredrick's handsome squire, Bowan. Velena could hardly blame him; Daisy was, indeed, a very attractive girl. At sixteen, she was full figured, with honey-blond hair pulled back into a long thin plait[7] that hung past her waist. She had blue eyes and a heart-shaped face that dimpled when she smiled.

It was early yet, and not time for supper, but Lord Rolland, wishing to refresh his lord and company after their long journey, served them all hot-spiced wine and wastel, a fine white bread reserved for the upper classes. Velena broke off a piece and brought it to her mouth, letting it melt on her tongue.

It'd been more than two weeks since she'd had such good bread to eat. But her momentary lapse into ecstasy was short lived, as

Lord Rolland seated himself next to her father at the dais, where she found herself forced to endure, once again, the memories of their losses at Landerhill, as her father relayed to Lord Rolland all pertinent news, including that of the death of Baroness Cecilia Ambrose.

Velena continued to pick at her bread, but it had lost its flavor, as her mind wandered back into the blackness of that day. She wanted to get up and leave, but it wouldn't have been appropriate for her to do so.

Fortunately for her, the conversation between her father and his bailiff was cut short by the ruckus entering the hall in the form of her father's knights and squires chanting loudly, "No brown bread, no bran; no wheat bread, no game; but bring us in good ale, just bring us the good ale; for our blessed Lady's sake, bring us some ale!"

All present burst into applause and laughter, joining in the chant, and from that moment until the noon meal was served and consumed, Velena was able to remain moderately distracted as the hall came alive with noise and revelry.

---

[7] **Dais:** A raised platform used for a speaker, seats of honor, or a throne.

[8] **Plait:** A braid (pronounced "plat").

forgiven

The gravel crunched beneath their feet as Lord Rolland led Sir Richard, Velena, and Daisy out of the hall. Snow had just begun to dust the ground. Daisy kept glancing behind her as they walked, gaining Velena's notice so that she followed Daisy's gaze back to the hall steps where Squire Bowan stood, now joined by a young boy who seemed to be peppering him with questions.

Velena leaned in so only Daisy could hear her, "He certainly is handsome."

"Who?"

"Who, indeed. The man with the matching dimples. Heaven knows what your children would look like."

At the mention of children, Daisy blushed a deep red. "I wish I knew his name. I was too embarrassed to inquire."

"I wasn't."

"My lady?"

Velena looked back as the men walked on before them. Confident their conversation was being ignored, she continued, "Bowan Rawling, Squire to Sir Fredrick Rawling, his uncle."

Daisy looked as though she'd been handed a gift. "Bowan. It's such a handsome name. I've always thought names should match up with how a person looks, don't you?"

"I don't see how that can be accomplished, seeing as how we're born and named all looking much the same."

"Oh, I disagree, my lady. I've seen some very ugly babies."

Velena covered her mouth to stifle a laugh, catching the attention of the men preceding them.

"And how did you find your meal, Lady Velena?"

Velena moved her hand to her stomach, "It's been weeks since I've eaten so fine a meal. It was heavenly, Lord Rolland, truly."

Daisy nodded in agreement.

Rolland smiled, "I'm happy to see you well satisfied; from what your father's told me, you've had a…a difficult journey. I've been wanting to offer you my sympathies."

"Not at all. The constant jostling of the wagon took its toll, but I'm no worse for it," Velena answered, smiling politely without meeting anyone's eyes, except Daisy's, who looked reprovingly at her.

Rolland looked to Lord Richard and smiled awkwardly. "Well, I…I know you must be anxious to have an account of the castle, but I thought I'd take the liberty of having a bath set up for you in your solar first. The water's being heated now; it shouldn't take too long."

Sir Richard looked at his daughter and frowned before returning his attention to Lord Rolland. "Ah, thank you. There's no doubt of us needing one; I'm thinking Velena might enjoy the first use of it, though. I'd like to look around at the rest of the grounds now and see how things have fared in my absence."

Velena smiled her thanks, but it didn't reach her eyes.

"I'll see to it that some curtains are hung for her privacy. If you'll excuse me, I'll meet you back at the keep," Lord Rolland said. He then gave a slight bow and walked away, leaving them to a rare moment of privacy…almost.

"Daisy, my dear, now would be a good time for you to see to Velena's trunk. Bring what she needs down to the bath."

"Yes, my lord."

Alone, Sir Richard turned to face his daughter, "Walk with me Velena; there are things we need to discuss."

"Such as?"

"Such as, why you chose to ignore Rolland's kind remarks."

"I didn't ignore him; I answered him."

"He was referring to the death of your mother, not to your bumpy ride. But I think you knew that."

Velena looked down as they walked, "I didn't...I don't want to talk about it with him."

"Does that go for me as well? You've barely said more than a handful of words to me since we left Landerhill."

Velena was quiet.

"Have you grieved for your mother?"

"Not as you have." It was simply said, but there was something in her tone that accused him.

Lord Richard stopped their walk in front of the granary, "You're angry with me?"

Velena wanted to take back what she'd said, and wondered if it was too late to placate him, but she loved her father, and the rift growing between them was growing more painful every day. How honest should she be? "You would have left me," she finally blurted out.

"I don't understand."

"You tried to get into mother's room—I watched you. If you'd succeeded, you'd be dead. You'd both be dead! And...and I...I'd be alone. You didn't care that I'd be alone." Velena began to weep and her father's heart broke at her confession.

"You were only thinking of her, and I was just so...so angry that you were willing to leave me behind."

The Baron quickly gathered his daughter into his arms and held her close, speaking into the dark brown tresses of her hair. "Oh, Daughter. I'm so sorry—so very sorry. It's too easy to get lost in one's own grief and to forget the sufferings of others, but you have to understand. Your mother was like air to me, and I've been in such a fog ever since her death," he confessed, letting his own tears spill down his unshaven cheeks. "I've even been angry at her for leaving me—so I understand you feeling the same way. Can you forgive me?"

If Lord Richard thought this would soothe his crying child, he was mistaken, for it only opened up the floodgates even more. Not knowing what to do or say, he led her behind the granary to shield her from prying eyes. He raised her chin and smiled sadly into her jewel colored eyes, glistening with tears, "Does this mean you don't forgive me?"

"Of course I forgive you! But I need your forgiveness as well. I saw your pain. I watched as you laid by her door, but I was afraid. You needed me, and I was too much of a coward to go to you. I've hated myself for it! What penance can I do for such a sin?"

"There was no sin in it—and you're not a coward."

"Yes, I am. People scare me. Someone here is diseased; I just know it! When we were at Landerhill, I had nightmares every night. I woke up every morning waiting for the first screams and moans of someone dying! I know I should be relieved that we're here, but I'm afraid. You asked me in my solar if I'd stand or fall—I fell, and continue to do so. What do I do now?" Velena choked.

"You'll get back up," Lord Richard said, as he gathered his daughter to his chest, stroking her hair and laying kisses upon the top of her head. He cursed the Plague for the havoc it continued to wreak upon his family, as Velena shook her head in denial. "Come now, we all fall, but it's our determination to get back up again that sets us apart."

"You're not disappointed in me?"

"Not in a hundred years."

"Oh Father, I love you so much!"

"And I, you."

"I miss Mother."

"So do I."

brother daniel

A young, thin-faced Friar Oshua fought sleep as he sat cross-legged in the corner watching Friar Daniel pace back and forth in the simply furnished stone room. To describe the room would not be to describe much, for it was void of anything save what was necessary for a daily life of sacrificial living—plus a few books.

His most important book lay open before Tristan, who sat at the room's only desk, in the room's only chair. The sixteen-year-old Studium Generale student flexed his fingers through a fist full of unkempt brown hair, as his blue gray eyes went from one end of the page to the other.

He read aloud, "*In principio erat Verbum et Verbum erat apud Deum et Deus...*"

Friar Oshua clucked his tongue as Friar Daniel interrupted him abruptly, "Speak French, brother. In England, the common man speaks French. When we read the Holy Scriptures, it should be in French. If it's not read to the common man in the common tongue to be understood..."

"There's no point in reading it," Friar Oshua inserted, having heard this speech before.

"You mock me, but you know I'm right." Friar Daniel's voice was firm, but kind.

His habit was to speak softly, but Tristan could tell he was starting to work himself up as he began quoting from memory in French. "*In the beginning was the Word, and the Word was with God, and the*

Word was God. He was in the beginning with God. All things came into being through Him and apart from Him nothing came into being that has come into being. In Him was life, and the life was the Light of men. The Light shines in the darkness and the darkness did not comprehend it..." the friar's voice trailed off as he stood motionless before the room's only window.

Tristan could see the gravity of those words in the friar's young eyes. He was only twenty-one, but he was wise beyond his years. His every breath was breathed only for God, and there was no one in the world Tristan respected more. He waited patiently for him to continue, but from his spot on the floor, Friar Oshua felt differently.

"Brother Daniel, pray tell, are you planning to continue?"

The silent friar turned from his reverie and smiled at Tristan. "Read on."

Tristan continued where the friar had left off, easily translating the Latin into French. *"There came a man sent from God whose name was John. He came as a witness, to testify about the Light, so that all might believe through him."* Tristan stopped here. "Isn't this proof of our need for priests? Through Saint John the Baptist, men came to Christ."

"We are, all of us who know and belong to Christ, saints; remember that. That is why I can call you brother. But read on starting here, and your question will be answered." Tristan waited for the friar to remove his finger.

"But as many as received Him, to them He gave the right to become children of God, even to those who believe in His name, who were born, not of blood nor of the will of the flesh nor of the will of man, but of God."

"You see there, not of the will of flesh nor of the will of man. Do see you it?" Brother Daniel asked, his boyishly handsome features growing ever more animated.

He continued, "Man cannot, nor has he ever had the capabilities to secure anyone's entrance into Heavenly places. We can't even do it ourselves, for that matter, *it is the gift of God; not as a result of works, so that anyone can boast. For we are His workmanship, created in Christ Jesus for good works, which God prepared beforehand so that we would walk in them.* This is in Ephesians; turn there. Oh, brother Tristan, there are so many amazing treasures the apostle Paul has left us with to find." Again the friar indicated where Tristan should begin reading, and then returned to his excited pacing.

"He chose us in Him before the foundation of the world, that we would be holy and blameless before Him. In love He predestined us to adoption as sons through Jesus Christ to Himself, according to the kind intention of His will, to the praise of the glory of His grace, which He freely bestowed on us in the Beloved. In Him we have redemption through His blood, the forgiveness of our trespasses, according to the riches of His grace, which He lavished on us."

"Stop! There is more—oh, so much more! But let us think on this first. If we were chosen before the foundations of the world— before the foundations of the world! Think of that! How then could any priest dare tell you it is not so! Or tell you it *is* so, for that matter! What rightful authority have they been given to excommunicate a man's soul? Or...or...or to issue indulgences assuring him of his place in Heaven. To charge money for salvation—it's evil!"

"Amen," piped up Friar Oshua.

"Amen!" Friar Daniel reiterated. "To hear their confessions and forgive them, as if they were able to stand in the place of the Holy Spirit, Himself. Only God can save!"

The friar stopped his pacing, and smiling from ear to ear, he thumped his fist upon the desk, "What think you of that, brother Tristan?"

"I cannot refute it, but I wonder that you say such things, when you, yourself, hear the confessions of men?"

"It's true I hear them. It brings men comfort because it's what they know, but they don't receive the forgiveness they seek through me. I count myself blessed that I can use that wonderful time of intimacy to direct them to God. I used to believe that the office of priest was essential for the saving of a man's soul. But then the more I read, the more I was convinced that the office of priest is met in our Lord Jesus Christ, and in Him alone. Much is said of that in Hebrews."

"And the church? What role does it have then?"

"The church then or the church now?" The friar let out an exasperated sigh and joined the now sleeping Oshua on the floor beneath the window opposite Tristan. "Scripture says that *they were continually devoting themselves to the apostles teaching and to fellowship, to the breaking of bread and to prayer.*"

"And you don't think they are doing this now?" Tristan asked, crossing his arms, and reclining his chair back onto two legs against the wall.

"You must look closely...*devoting themselves to the apostles teaching*. That's in Acts of the Apostles. Their teaching is what you now hold in your hands. But you are one in a thousand. The church keeps the Holy Scriptures to themselves when they teach in Latin. How many laymen do you know who understand Latin?"

"None." Friar Oshua said, not bothering to open his eyes.

"Few. You, me, and the nobles if they feel it necessary to devote themselves to such things. We are the privileged few when you consider the mass of unlearned villeins and yeomen[9] who surround us. *All Scripture is inspired by God and profitable for teaching, for reproof, for correction, for training in righteousness, so that the man of God may be adequate, equipped for every good work.* The same good works mentioned afore—the very ones that God almighty has prepared for us beforehand! And yet! These Scriptures—these very inspired words of God—are kept from the people. Tell me, how is the church then fulfilling its role? The Scriptures should be given in our native tongue for all to read or..."

"There's no point in reading it," Friar Oshua repeated, smiling to himself.

Daniel laughed. "Well, if it's worth saying once, it's worth saying twice. Do you have any actual sleeping you plan on doing?"

"Keep talking and I'll get there."

Tristan laughed at the pair of them. "What you say is true, brother Daniel, but most can't read."

"And that is why I read it to them." He reached his arm up from where he was still seated on the floor, twisting his hand around to point all five fingers out the window as if palming an imaginary ball.

"Those people—God's people—are living in the shadow of a *great* and *glorious* self-righteous church. Its arms are far reaching, leading all manner of souls into a great darkness." He pointed at his chest. "I feel this darkness! It's a burden to me." Tristan leaned his chair forward and waited for the friar to continue; tears were in the friar's eyes. "But I know the joy that could be theirs. I found it on my hands and knees; and the only priest to hear my confessions was the Great High Priest, who's great and mighty outstretched arms reach even further, spanning the distance to lead even the most un-worthiest of sinners back into His gracious embrace. Hebrews again," he said gesturing towards the Scriptures.

Tristan looked around nervously, as if half expecting the Pope, himself, to enter the room and condemn the poor friar for speaking unforgivable blasphemies. "Aren't you afraid of defying the church?"

At that, the friar laughed heartily. *"Do not fear those who kill the body but are unable to kill the soul; but rather fear Him who is able to destroy both soul and body in hell.* It's in St. Matthew, but it was our Lord Jesus who said so. I'll tell you something, Tristan, when I took my orders to become a friar, it was for less than virtuous reasons. Being shoved out the door for noble ones will be my honor."

"But if the church was to excommunicate you, wouldn't it greatly hinder your ministry? You'd have all the credibility of a fool preaching heresy. Don't misunderstand me, I'm not telling you to withhold the truth, but perhaps just not to shout it from your window."

Both men looked to Friar Oshua for some sort of sarcasm, but were only met with snores. With that brother Daniel stood up and spread his arms wide, his voice barely a whisper.

"Haven't you discerned what God is doing? He's excommunicating *us*. Mankind is dropping like flies—for our hypocrisy, for our blaspheming, for our negligence of His Holy Word. The irony of it all amazes me still! The world *is* being judged—the church is being judged. There's no mistaking it."

"We're doomed then."

"No. There will be a remnant. There's always a remnant." Friar Daniel walked slowly over to Tristan and closed the Bible. "Time is of the essence, Brother Tristan. Don't waste it being afraid. I'm sorry that this will be our last meeting," he said.

"So am I…I could never thank you enough for all…"

At that moment, there was a knock on the door, quickly followed by the face of a teenage boy still in his novice year of joining the order. "There's a woman here who wishes to speak with Lord Tristan."

"A woman?" Tristan sat perplexed.

"Show her in Brother Finlae," Friar Daniel said without skipping a beat, "also bring in Brother Oshua's chair, so she might be seated with Brother Tristan."

Friar Daniel then shook his sleeping friend awake. "Get up, Brother Oshua; we're receiving a visitor."

"He'll never know I'm here," he mumbled groggily.

"It's a woman."

"I'll be in my room." With that, he was up and out, leaving Brother Daniel and Tristan to share in a laugh at his expense.

"Brother Oshua took up orders because he's afraid of women," Brother Daniel explained.

Tristan laughed, but looked down sheepishly. "He's not the only one."

---

[9] **Yeomen:** A commoner, cultivating a small land estate; a freeholder.

tragedy

Brother Finlae returned a moment later wearing a look of apology. "I beg your pardon, Lord Tristan, but she refuses to come in. Instead, she wishes me to say that her business with you is urgent and to please come outside."

"Thank you, Brother Finlae, lead the way."

"We'll all go out together," Brother Daniel said, taking note of Tristan's uneasy demeanor.

Tristan walked out onto the lawn, squinting against the bright of day as his eyes adjusted to being indoors for so long. "Lady Agnes? What are you doing here? Where's my mother?"

Lady Isabelle's traveling companion, who was also her first cousin, stood before them visibly shaken and crying.

"What's wrong?" Tristan made a motion as if to touch her arm, but the woman jerked away.

"Don't touch me, Lord Tristan. I'm unclean, I'm sure of it," she said, crossing herself with her hand.

At this point, Tristan became visibly frustrated and dispensed with all formality. "Agnes! Where's my mother?"

"She's at the house, my lord; we arrived not but an hour ago. She's dying! There I've said it plainly." With that Agnes' tears turned to choking sobs. "My poor cousin!"

"She's dy—what of my sisters?"

Lady Agnes tried to stay the tide of tears with the hem of her cloak, but was unsuccessful. "Already dead, my lord. Oh, Tristan! I'm so sorry…so very sorry." Tristan felt light headed as Agnes continued to blubber. "Lady Ann and Lady Alice died at your aunts' house in London—along with your uncle and your cousin, Henry. Young Mary died on the way here. Your mother refused to leave her on the side of the road, and so the driver just got out and left us."

"And now?"

"She's still in the back of the wagon. The servants have all run off, and there's no one to bury her. Please don't ask me to do the job. I'll not touch her!"

"Well someone had better!" he shouted. "How dare you leave her out in the open to be scavenged by birds." Brother Daniel laid a hand on Tristan's trembling shoulder. He settled, but began to pull at his hair, not knowing what else to do with himself.

Brother Daniel finally spoke up. "This woman's frantic with grief; to berate her won't bring back your sisters—nor heal your mother."

"I must go to her."

"That you mustn't do, Lord Tristan, "Lady Anges whimpered, "She was adamant that you not come."

"Of course I'm going. I can't just leave her to die alone," he said, not knowing if he actually had the courage to do so.

"No, you mustn't. She forbids it! It's her earnest wish that you make haste to Wineford Castle as planned, and be with your uncle." Agnes pulled a moneybag from beneath her cloak and tossed it at his feet, not daring to approach him. "Here. It's from your desk."

No one knew how the dreaded contagion was circulated, but it was believed that even touching the clothing of an infected person would mean one's death. And Lady Agnes, who'd already touched her mistress upon helping her out of the wagon, did not want to chance that Tristan would suffer the same fate as she felt certain would be hers.

"She told me to tell you how much she loves you, and begs only that I bring back someone to whom she can make confession."

Tristan stood rooted to the ground, mute and barely able to compute what was being said. Without warning, he turned and strode back towards the small room from whence he'd come.

Brother Daniel remained. "Dear woman, rest yourself. I'll accompany you to your mistress, myself, only allow me first to get the young master on his way."

"God bless you, Friar!" she cried, crossing herself again and clasping her hands together, as tears streamed freely down her face. "Only make haste, I beg you."

The friar nodded.

Back inside the stone room, Tristan stood gripping the opposing sides of the small desk. The door hinges creaked as the friar entered from behind him; the friar said nothing, but waited for Tristan to acknowledge his presence.

"How can one moment change a person's life so completely?" he finally uttered.

"God uses many moments for many different purposes. And sometimes the changes that those moments bring are for our good. In fact, we know they are, *to those who love Him and are called according to His purposes.*"

"Ephesians?" Tristan questioned, picking at a splinter coming loose from the wood.

"Romans."

"Do you believe that?"

"With all my heart," Brother Daniel said, thinking it best to say no more on the subject but inwardly praying that Tristan's faith would not be shaken. "Let's get you to your uncle's."

"I've nothing with me. Just my horse."

"And this." Daniel approached him from the side and pressed the moneybag into Tristan's hand. "Come, the Brothers will supply the rest."

"I should go to her."

"Listening to confessions is my job—you said it yourself."

Tristan came back to life. "You'll die."

"I'd already determined to stay and care for the sick. Their bodies are dying; they need not lose their souls in the process. If the Lord is patient, I'll go and give your mother the truth of God's salvation."

"I don't know what to say."

"*Thank you*, will suffice." Brother Daniel smiled.

In record time, Tristan's horse was loaded with food and blankets. Having been joined by Brother Oshua, they stood just outside the stables. Tristan mounted and looked down at the friars. "It shouldn't be this way."

Brother Daniel only smiled. "It's for me to stay and for you to go; carry the Truth with you. And remember the words of Saint Paul, that *we have boldness and confident access through faith in Him. Therefore, I ask you not to lose heart at my tribulations on your behalf, for they are your glory.*"

"Ephesians?"

"Ephesians." Brother Daniel grinned. "A fitting farewell, I thought."

"Very fitting. Please..." Tristan fought to stay in control. "Tell my mother I love her, and...and that I'm sorry I..."

The handsome friar looked up at him and gripped his arm in understanding.

Tristan wiped his nose with his sleeve, as he focused his eyes towards his westward destination. "I feel so alone."

Brother Oshua approached him, taking firm hold of his hand. "A common ailment among men, unfortunately. But I know for a fact that Brother Daniel has included something in your saddlebags that should help with that. God be with you, Tristan," he said, exchanging a look with Friar Daniel who only nodded solemnly.

Brother Oshua slapped the horses' flank, signaling that the time had come for him to be on his way. It broke into a trot taking Tristan towards the edge of town. He turned in his saddle to see Brother Daniel's arm raised high, "Keep the faith, Brother! God is still good!" he called out to him.

Together, the friars watched him ride off, each one praying for the future of the young man—and for the future of a dying world.

Finally, Friar Daniel called out towards the house, "Brother Finlae, please fetch the Lady Agnes. We're ready to go." His voice was confident, but there was a look of finality in his eyes. "You don't have to come with me Oshua."

"Someone's got to dig your grave."

Brother Daniel shook his head in amusement. "You know, I'm not sure that becoming a friar was the best occupational choice for you."

"You couldn't be more right."

tristan

Velena was the last to arrive at the great hall. The food had already reached the tables, and Lord Rolland and her father were engaged in a discussion concerning some business they had to attend to for the day.

Velena took her seat. "Forgive me, Father. I didn't hear the call to eat."

"Didn't hear it?"

"I was asleep."

"In the middle of the day? You're still not sleeping at night?"

Velena looked down, trying to cover a telltale yawn, "It's alright."

"No, it's not," Sir Richard said, with concern.

"Some hot goat's milk before bed, perhaps," Lord Rolland interjected. "My mother used to give me some when I was a boy, and it worked wonders—from what I remember anyway. I haven't been a boy in more years then I care to admit," he said with a laugh, stroking the graying growth of his beard.

"There's still plenty of brown in there," Sir Richard said with a chuckle, motioning with his hand for Daisy to approach the dais. "Look here at this, it's only the lightness of my beard that manages to hide mine."

So began a mirthful war of who was graying more until Lord Richard turned to a waiting Daisy.

"You have need of me, my lord?" she inquired.

"Yes, Daisy, from now on, I want Velena to have something hot to drink before bed until you find the drink that sets her to sleep peacefully. Start with goat's milk; I'll leave it to you to make sure the kitchen sets it aside for her. If that doesn't work, try spiced wine, and so on. Her inability to sleep is affecting her health—and her appetite."

Daisy turned to Velena to see her picking at her food, "Aye, my lord, she grows thin; I can attest to that."

"I'm right here, you know," Velena protested.

"I know where you are," Sir Richard quipped back at his daughter, "and I'm making sure you're taken care of, as is a father's duty."

There was nothing else for Velena to do but submit, for truly her night had been a fitful one. She was ready to take any suggestion that was offered or forced upon her, as the case may be. She was at her wits end, and could barely keep her eyes open even now. She laid a hand across her mouth, trying to stifle another yawn.

She'd been chasing sleep ever since her first night out of the forest, and every night was the same, insomnia followed by a rotation of unpleasant dreams, followed by insomnia. She'd been prepared for this very thing last night when she'd seen the glow of a candle creep past the cracks around her door.

As she had nothing better to do then to stare into darkness for the next couple of hours, she'd crawled out of bed to investigate, careful not to wake Daisy. Pulling her robe up over her shoulders, she'd peeked out her door to see a house servant leading a young man down the hall by candle light.

"I beg your pardon, Lord Rolland," Velena interrupted, "but I wonder that your nephew isn't with us this afternoon. I'm happy not to be the only tardy one. I suppose his journey must have been an especially tiring one."

"He's not yet arrived, Lady Velena—tonight, though. I expect him and his mother to arrive late this evening, along with his three sisters. You girls will finally have someone else to chitter about with,

Lord help us." Lord Rolland chuckled before taking in a large bite of fish tart.

Velena felt a chill go down her spine. Could it be that an unknown or unexpected guest had been let into the house? Who knows where he could have come from. What if he was sick when he arrived, and the reason he wasn't here with them now was because he was, in fact, now dead in the room from Plague! Velena began to feel the blood rushing into her ears, but forced herself to remain composed.

Perhaps there was a better explanation, which at this point would be any explanation at all. "Excuse my confusion, but what guest was let into the solar down the hall from mine? It was meant to be for my brother, and though absent, I don't suppose just anyone would be admitted." She hoped.

She was answered by two blank stares.

"It was in the middle of the night, I…I assumed it was your nephew. Who else would be shown to the second floor?"

Lord Richard released Lord Rolland from the table so that he could look into the matter, and then went back to his eating. "Don't fret, Rolland will get it sorted out."

After supper, as they were leaving the hall, the bailiff returned to meet them. He was composed, but the eyes Velena found so wonderful, were now red rimmed and glossy. He confirmed without delay that Tristan was, in fact, last night's mystery guest, and then asked Lord Richard for a private audience. Velena caught no more than a glimpse of the bailiff for the rest of the day.

Though curious about Lord Rolland's obvious distress, she was relieved to find out it was his nephew that occupied the room and not some sick traveler after all. She busied herself with spinning yarn, checking on the daily tasks of the servants, recruiting Daisy to take a walk with her around the pond, and other such equally mundane distractions. She sought out anything to keep her mind off of the world around her, finding reason to smile only once upon noticing a certain eight-year-old blond peeking out at her from behind the smithy.

She fully expected to bump into the bailiff's nephew, in passing at the very least, for there were not many places one could be alone at Wineford, but she didn't. So, the day wore on uneventful, threatening to end as dully as it had begun.

Velena ascended the wooden staircase of the keep, hot goat's milk in hand, hoping it would have the desired effect of helping her sleep. Her steps were slow and her thoughts muddled as she reached the top. She was getting a headache and the only thing she could get her mind to focus on was how much dust seemed to collect on the hem of her tunic when she didn't bother to lift it.

Absent-mindedly, she began tugging at her hairpins, hoping that she would relieve some of the pressure building around her temples. Long dark plaits began falling past her shoulders. She tucked the hairpins in between her lips as she loosened and combed through them with her free hand, until a noise coming from behind the door at the end of the hall caused her to pause. It was Rolland's nephew.

Her solar was to the left, but she found her thoughts going right. Then an idea, not quite her own, planted itself in her mind with such calling that she felt compelled to answer it at once. Setting her cup down at the top of the stairs so that she might move more quickly, she descended back down through the keep, and out towards the kitchen.

a visitor

Tristan hadn't left the upstairs room since arriving the night before. The gatekeeper recognized him and had shown him back to the keep. There, he was able to explain to the night guard, who also recognized him from previous visits he'd made to his Uncle Rolland, that he wanted to keep his arrival quiet until morning when he could speak to his uncle privately.

It was well that he did keep quiet. It proved a difficult enough task to tell one's uncle about the death of his sister and nieces without having to do it in the dead of night. If prodded, Tristan might have remembered from his uncle's letter that the Baron and his daughter were in the castle, and that it would have behooved him to pay homage, by way of even the smallest of greetings to express his gratitude at having been provided a chance at waiting out the terrible effects of the deadly Plague in his castle.

But life was cruel, and it was, after all, too late to escape the effects of death. He was now in no temper to see anyone, a baron or otherwise. So, instead, he'd curled up into the mental equivalent of a fetal position and sequestered himself inside the room, feeling at every moment that he was falling into a black hole that he'd never be able to emerge from.

It was now his second night in the castle, and he'd still not changed his clothes or taken any food. He was devoting himself entirely to the misery of his own company. He'd sat for hours at the only desk, staring at a large tapestry above his bed. Upon pain of death, he couldn't have given record of its color nor its depiction.

As time passed, Tristan experienced faces swimming past him, as if they were on a loop. There was the friar, all love and generosity, wise and sacrificial; his uncle and his expression of anguish at the mention of his sister's death; and his sweet, soft-spoken mother, quiet and gentle. His sisters next, one by one they floated by—until one more face hovered past him—Gwenhavare. She'd been approaching the church at the edge of town just as he was leaving the Brothers.

He'd danced with her at a party once, and then spent the better part of the evening in her company. He thought her beautiful—in face and character. She'd been easy to talk to, which had been a relief to Tristan, who was generally shy of women, and so he thought she must be the most delightful creature he'd ever met.

So frustratingly, as he'd ridden past, he'd done little more than nod in her direction. He'd still been in shock over the news of his mother and sisters. He remembered how Gwenhavare had looked confused and hurt. Tristan justified his actions by telling himself that he'd never see her again anyway, but he wasn't truly certain about anything, and so he prayed. Fervently, he tried to devote himself to prayer, to shut out the faces, but relief wouldn't come, and his frustration only grew.

He felt tortured; he arose from his chair so abruptly that it fell backward, sounding a loud thud that reverberated across the stone floor. He'd hung several heavy satchels over the back of the chair when he first arrived, so they too landed on the floor in a great heap. Tristan stared at the pile the way he'd stared at the tapestries.

Time went by unnoticed until he finally decided that the mental effort to get to his bed was more important than the mental effort of picking up the chair. It'd be there in the morning. So, still fully clothed, he'd no sooner laid his head upon his pillow than he heard a soft knock at his door.

A dull moan escaped his lips. Perhaps his uncle had returned and wanted to speak with him. Tristan opened the door, not to the masculine and well-weathered face of his uncle, as he'd expected, but to a lovely young woman with green eyes and dark hair cascading in tangled waves over her shoulders. She held a trencher full of food and wore an apologetic expression, that consequently, went rather well with the dark blue of her gown.

"Lady Velena."

"You recognize me?"

"You're too young to be the Baron's wife."

Velena's smile faded slightly at the mention of her mother, "It's been a while hasn't it?"

"Five years."

"Do I look different?"

"From a ten-year-old girl? Just a little." He smiled without actually feeling it.

"You too. May I come in?"

Tristan blinked at her boldness, but stepped aside.

"I asked the kitchen if you'd taken any food since arriving, and they said no, so I thought I'd bring you some. Are you feeling poorly?"

"Uh. Have you talked with my uncle yet?"

"No. He hid himself sometime after supper."

"Oh."

"It must run in the family."

"What's that?"

"Hiding."

"It must be a Blakely trait. But I'm only half Blakely, so it appears I'm not very good at it."

"How so?"

"You found me."

"You were noisy. Your mother and sisters must be better at it; I've still yet to find them. I was under the impression that they were going to be traveling with you. I hope they arrive shortly; it'll be nice to have other women around."

Tristan turned away from her and sat down upon the bed with his back up against the wall, arms resting on bent knees. *Of all the questions to ask me.* Small talk was one thing, but she'd only been in the room two minutes and he found himself cornered into bearing his soul.

Frankly, he was surprised that he could even make small talk when only moments ago he'd been ready to bed down into unconscious oblivion. He really needed to be unconscious. He looked up at Velena, confident that she was sincere in her ignorance, and he felt sorry for the embarrassment he would cause her once he explained things.

He wasn't sure just how he managed it, but his words began to flow, swift and to the point. "My mother's dead, actually—or...or perhaps still dying. She arrived home from my aunts' house sick from the Plague. My three younger sisters died before she arrived—as did my aunt's husband and a cousin. She sent word to me that I wasn't to go back home, but to leave directly for my uncle's, or rather your father's castle. In either case, I left without seeing her or being able to say goodbye. So here I am. The moment I arrived, I knew what lousy company I'd be, so I thought it best to sequester myself in here and spare you all the burden of speaking with me."

Velena stood aghast. "Tristan, I...I should have thought before I spoke." She floundered, wondering if she should even bother trying to apologize or if it would better serve them both if, she just turned and ran for her room, avoiding him for the rest of her life.

But wise or foolish, her feet remained stubbornly planted. "My mother died too," she blurted out. "I should have known. I'm...I'm so sorry. I wasn't thinking."

"Baroness Ambrose is gone?"

"Yes."

"Didn't you have a brother?"

"Yes—Britton. He's in Calais." Velena hung her head and began looking everywhere but at Tristan, her gaze finally coming to rest on the overturned chair. Tristan noticed.

He pushed himself up from the bed, "Oh, I...I knocked it over. I should have picked it up."

Velena set the food she'd been holding on the desk and bent

down to help gather up the satchels as Tristan picked up the chair. "Go ahead and set them on the desk," he said.

"What's this?"

"What?"

"This book. It fell out of your bag." Velena bent down and retrieved the black leather bound book still laying on the floor.

Tristan stood dumbfounded, extending his hand to accept it from her. *"Take the Truth with you,"* Friar Daniel had said.

There was something in the way that Tristan looked at the book, as if it were something most precious, that made Velena feel doubly self-conscious for the way she'd intruded upon him.

She didn't wait for him to answer, but felt it was now time to make her escape. "I hope that you'll be able to eat something. And again, I'm so very…very sorry for your loss…losses—and for my rude intrusion." Velena turned to leave.

Tristan looked up. "No, I'm…I'm not offended. Truly, it was vain of me to think I was the only one suffering. I'm sorry about your mother—and thank you for the food," he finished lamely.

"You're welcome," Velena replied, unable to stop thinking about what an idiot she'd made of herself.

Tristan held no such thoughts of her.

regrets

Velena retreated from Tristan's presence, feeling the fool for adding to his pain with her thoughtlessness. She entered into her solar, slipped off her shoes and tossed them angrily against the far wall. They cast a flutter of shadows as they clattered to the floor.

The hearth fire burned brightly, pushing the chill from the room. Then moving toward her bed, Velena let her mind drift through memories of her mother and brother, until at random, her thoughts began turning to Peter. *Was he still alive?*

She soon became restless and realized that she was still dressed. The room was growing dim as the fire began to wane. *Where was Daisy, anyway?* With some effort, and much fumbling with the buttons at her wrists, she managed to shimmy out of her clothing, herself.

The room was now also cold. Velena threw a few logs onto the fire and looked towards the layers of blankets that hugged her bed and grimaced. Her bed may mean warmth, but it wouldn't mean sleep. Velena turned away and grabbed for her robe instead, before facing the gilded mirror hanging above the modestly sized vanity. Her reflection was inviting. She was almost sixteen and in her prime; she should be getting her own home ready for a night of slumber. She should be climbing into bed beside her husband.

Once again she wondered if Peter would wait for her. She tried to picture him there—bidding her to join him beneath the covers. Her mind wandered as her fingers moved deftly through her rich brown tresses, combing, separating and overlapping until she'd formed one long plait. Throwing it over her shoulder, she placed her nightcap on her head and went looking for her book, *Tristan and Isulte*. If sleep wouldn't be caught, then she wouldn't bother chasing it.

"There has to be a candle around here somewhere," she spoke into the empty room.

The door flung open and in flew Daisy holding Velena's, now half empty, cup of cold goat's milk. "You left this on the top of the stairs, I presume."

"Ugh, so much for my good night's sleep. I forgot all about it. I was trying to find a candle so that I could read in bed."

"I'm ever so sorry, but I was up here earlier and noticed that we hadn't any candles, not that I was surprised, seeing as how we've been letting them burn down to nothing every night. So I went in search of more, but I couldn't find one! So I asked one of the servants where they were kept, but when I got to the spot where they were supposed to be, there were no candles in sight. I went back and asked him for more help, and he was horrid rude about it. They turned up not where they should have been, but somewhere entirely different. He didn't even apologize for treating me like some sort of ninny who doesn't know what's what or what's where."

Velena climbed into bed with her book as Daisy continued on in her twittery sort of tirade, lighting a candle and placing it beside the bed before removing her own clothing. Her rant finally ended as she slipped inside her cocoon of blankets on the trundle below.

By the end of it, Velena had gone from irritated to amused. She looked down affectionately at Daisy, "Is that all?"

"Is what all?" Daisy let go a yawn.

"No more to complain about?"

"I kicked over your milk as I came up the stairs."

"I'm sorry." Velena giggled.

"No you're not. How'd you go about leaving it there anyway?"

"I left it there on my way down to get Tristan some food. I meant to come back for it"

Daisy gasped and turned over to face Velena, "Oh, my lady,

you saw him? Did you hear what became of his mother and sisters? What a tragedy!"

"I know—now, but only because he told me. It would have been good information for you to have shared with me before I walked into his room."

"You went in his room—alone?"

"I would have taken you with me, but you were nowhere to be found. You've been disappearing at every opportunity today. Where were you anyway?"

"Looking for candles."

"Before that."

Daisy dimpled, "Watching Bowan train with Roger Longfellow."

"Well stop it—you're my lady's maid, not his."

Daisy smiled up at the warm glow of light haloing her mistress's face, knowing her reprimand was nothing more than a slap on the wrist. "Yes, my lady," she said, her voice muffled beneath the covers she was holding up above her mouth to hide her smile.

Velena rolled her eyes as she raised her book up in an effort to catch the candle light. *Tristan and Isulte*, read the words printed clearly across the cover. *Tristan.* Just reading his name brought a new wave of embarrassment. Tossing the book to the end of her bed, she turned and blew out the candle.

melancholy

Over the course of the next week, Velena and Tristan crossed paths seldom and spoke even less. For living in a place where there was little chance of privacy, they seemed to manage it just fine. Each of them was trying not to tread on the grief of the other as best as possible.

As for Velena, sorrow continually resurfaced, as an unshakable melancholy began to set in. She rarely said more than absolutely necessary to Daisy and began avoiding her father for fear that he'd see her despair.

For Daisy, it had been days past feeling sympathetic towards her mistress's somber mood swings. She'd grown tired of being cooped up inside while Velena sat silently with her book. On one occasion, she'd finally managed to coax her out for a walk through the orchards, but to Velena the winter trees looked dead, and it was an awful reminder of what loomed beyond the castle walls. After that, Daisy had to resort to begging. "My lady, please can't we go outside?"

"It's too cold; I don't want to go outside."

"I'm going crazy in here!" She fell back upon the bed in exasperation. "I can only spin so much thread."

"Read a book."

"That's a fine thing to say when you've got the only one."

Velena got up from the small desk and tossed her book at Daisy. "Happy?"

"No."

"You're getting impertinent."

"And you're shriveling up. You need fresh air, my lady—we both do." Daisy got up and grabbed onto Velena's hands, "Please, a short walk to the stables. You can look at the horses, and maybe go for a ride."

"I don't want to ride…"

"Just look then."

Velena's shoulders sagged. "Alright."

"Alright?"

"Do you want to go or not?" Velena said, wrapping herself up in her fur trimmed cloak.

Daisy let out a delighted squeal and led the way out of the keep before Velena had a chance to change her mind.

Velena padded after Daisy through a blanket of white powder, not a bit surprised to find more than just horses occupying the stable yard. For snow or no snow, an elaborate, and rather odd looking, wood and metal quintain had been set up only a stone's throw away.

A very enthusiastic Sir Fredrick sat on the ground manipulating the man-sized mechanism by way of ropes and pulleys as Bowan jumped, dodged, and blocked the attacks of the oncoming sandbag and shielded dummy arm, swinging from left to right and full circle. There were other squires standing by, of course, but no one else mattered to Daisy; she had eyes only for him. And, if it were possible for Velena to assess Bowan's returning her maid's affections by how high he began jumping once she came into view, then it could easily be said that their admiration for one another was mutual.

Velena didn't really mind Daisy's infatuation with the squire, truth be told. It was, in fact, very difficult for her to feel one way or another about anything when she felt mostly nothing at all.

"I'm going to do that one day."

Velena looked down to see a small boy addressing her. "Do what?"

"Fight."

"Oh, is that so?" she queried.

Yes, I'm going to be Bowan's page in two birthdays."

"Did he tell you that?"

"Yes."

"I see. Well, it's a lot of hard work, you know."

"I know all about hard work. My father's the smithy."

"I can tell," Velena said, thinking of the burly red-haired man who would probably never have to worry about losing his son in a crowd.

"My father made that," Jonas said, pointing.

"The quintain?"

"You already know what it's called? You're smart."

"Sometimes," Velena said, blowing warm air into her hands, "but I've never seen one that looks like that before. They're generally used for lance practice, are they not?"

The boy shrugged. "Sir Fredrick wanted him to make it that way. I don't know why."

Velena nodded, accepting the boys answer without further inquiry, before meandering her way amid the ring of onlookers. Undeterred, the boy followed her.

"Did you know I'm Jonas?"

"No, did you know that I'm Lady Velena?"

"Yes, and my sister knows too. Her name is Kat. Well, that's just what we call her. Her real name is…real name is…is…"

Velena smile, amusedly waiting for him spit it out.

"Her name is Katrina, but she likes Kat and…and Kitten— that's what Father calls her when he's not angry about something."

"Then for her sake, I hope she's an obedient girl." Velena paused to face him, realizing he wasn't going to go away on his own.

The boy shrugged. "She thinks you're really beautiful. She said that last time."

"And what do you think?" a deep voice interjected.

Young Jonas turned his freckled face to meet that of Sir Andret. "Oh, I don't like girls yet."

Andret chuckled, exchanging looks with Velena.

"My papa says they're nothing but...but...but trouble."

"I think he's right," he said with a wink, "especially this one, so you'd best be on your way." Andret made his best scary woman face and kicked at the boy's hind end. Jonas scampered just out of reach, giggling his way back into the crowd.

Velena stood transfixed at the sound of the five-year-old boy's mirthful and unadulterated laughter, allowing it to wash over her and to seep through the cracks of her defenses until despite herself, she smiled—and meant it. How had it not occurred to her that people could still be happy?

"Cute little mite."

"Yes," Velena agreed, pulling her cloak in tighter about her body. "Isn't it a bit cold out here to be practicing on that contraption?"

"Not unless you plan on sticking your tongue to it."

Velena delivered a small laugh that she thought would give his joke its proper due, but then excused herself politely, thinking she could go somewhere where she wouldn't have to make conversation.

"Oh, Father—I'm sorry," she said almost bumping into him as he came up to greet her. Velena was surprised to see that Tristan was with him.

"No need to apologize. I'm taking this young man out for a proper tour of the grounds; I thought you might like to join us."

"Oh, thank you but I...I promised Daisy I'd come out to the stables with her."

"Is that why you were walking back towards the keep?"

Velena looked at Tristan wondering if he could see through her pretenses. "I was just going to get my book. I was coming right back."

"Come, Daughter—no excuses today."

"But Daisy..."

"...is happily occupied, as anyone can see," he said with a

chuckle. "Just a short walk."

Velena gave an inward sigh, but obediently stepped into line beside them, stubbornly adding little more than infrequent nods and polite smiles to the ensuing conversation.

a beginning

During their walk, Tristan had taken some time to observe Lady Velena. He began realizing that he could no longer go on as he had been, and perhaps neither should she. So he found himself doing something he never imaged he'd do. Taking a deep breath, he knocked on her door.

"Come in," came the muffled answer.

Tristan hesitated a moment, knowing she wouldn't expect it to be him, but opened the door anyway. Velena stood by the hearth, her figure softly framed by the flickering glow of the fire. He had to admit she made a lovely picture. "Lady Velena?"

Velena startled, and then turned around to face him.

"Good Vespers to you."

A corner of her mouth rose at the strange greeting, and at him. His short cut sandy brown hair was standing on end as it usually did, presenting a comical look to an otherwise decidedly pleasant face, but it was his eyes that caught her attention. She'd noticed them before, but tonight they seemed especially beautiful. They had that same wonderful shape like his Uncle Rolland's, only they were blue instead of brown. They were also kind like his uncle's, except there was something more—something honest and disarming that immediately drove away some of the oppressive gloom from the room. Velena could literally feel it leaving.

Tristan flashed her an unsure smile, and then dove right in before losing his nerve, "I wanted to talk with you."

"I don't suppose you should be in here until Daisy comes back from the hall. I left early."

Tristan smiled at her double standards for room etiquette. "I know; I saw you leave. I was hoping to talk with you—alone."

Velena cocked her head to one side trying to ascertain what his intentions might be, but couldn't feel anything but at ease.

"Alright."

"I brought you this," he said, holding out a cup of something hot, "I never thanked you for the food you brought to me when I first arrived."

"You did thank me."

"Did I? Well, did I also tell you that although you satisfied my appetite, you forgot to bring me something to drink? I thought I could set the example for next time."

Velena accepted the cup from his hands and took a sip of the hot-spiced wine. "I apologize for my negligence," she simpered, "It won't happen again." Her relaxed and playful demeanor suited Tristan well, and gave him courage. "Please, sit."

Tristan looked around the room from the one chair at the desk to the bed at the other end. Unable to think of a better option, he sat down cross-legged in the middle of the floor.

Velena hesitated only a moment before joining him. She laughed, and their eyes locked in genuine pleasure, each enjoying the absurdity of the moment, as still another weight seemed to lift from her shoulders.

Tristan, who was normally given to a certain amount of shyness, especially around women, had mentally played out, over and over again, how this conversation might go, never really expecting to have made it past the door. Now, unexpectedly comfortable, he became even more confident in his purpose for being there.

"What did you want to tell me?"

"Just that, though I know my grief has been a difficult burden for me to bear, I've realized that it's not a burden unique only to me. I'm learning that there are many shades of sadness, and that the sadness of one can, in fact, affect the happiness of another. Unless, of course, neither are happy—in which case, could it be possible for happiness to be the product of two sad people finding each other?"

Velena shook her head slightly. "I don't understand."

"What I'm trying to say is that, I'm truly miserable in my present condition—but I think that you are too."

Velena saw his hands trembling in his lap as he continued pouring out his heart to her.

"I know that God has brought me here for a reason. He has…has allowed these things to happen to us, and I…I don't know why. I truly don't. I don't pretend to know His purposes, but one thing I do know is that in my misery, God has not allowed me to remain blind to the pain of others. I've been staying away from you because I didn't want to expose you to any further sorrow when you already had so much of your own. And it's definitely not my desire to have you walking on eggshells, worrying about what you might say to me, or hoping that I won't take offense at your words, or you at mine. The truth is…" Tristan took a deep breath. "I'm in sore need of company, and I was hoping that if we shared in each other's, we might have the benefit of being encouraged to…to live again."

Velena sat in disbelief! She'd never had a man talk to her this way. She dared not laugh, for his eyes told her that he was in earnest. Yes, they were the most honest eyes she'd ever seen, leaving her to think that his entire soul must be visible if only she were able to stare long enough. Suddenly, Velena realized she'd been staring, and not at all responding. She extended her hand. "I offer you my friendship freely." She felt the gentle squeeze of his hand in return.

As the moment passed, they both became aware of how silly they must look sitting cross-legged in the middle of the floor, and how inappropriate the situation would be should Daisy happen upon them.

"Well, I suppose I'd better go before I can't see my way back to my room."

"Just a moment, I'll get you a candle."

Tristan waited. "Thank you." He took the now lit candle from her hand and opened the door to leave. He was starting to feel embarrassed over his overt show of emotion. The conversation had gone favorably, but Velena had said very little, and he wondered if she was inwardly laughing at him.

"Tristan?"

"Yes."

"Would you like to do something tomorrow?"

"We could try our hand at the fish pond."

"Alright. Goodnight."

"Goodnight."

the dream

Tristan awoke the next morning, disoriented by his surroundings. It wasn't the first time that he had to remind himself that he wasn't in Oxfordshire with his mother and sisters. He hoped this disorientation would subside sooner rather than later.

He was still groggy as he ran his hands through his unkempt hair and swung his legs over the side of the bed, determined to make it out of the castle for his morning run. He walked over to the polished silver wall ornament that served as a makeshift mirror. His hair was unruly, but he liked it that way. He'd always been content to walk outside of everyone's notice if he could at all help it.

He dressed quickly, and exited his solar quietly before stopping at the basin in the hallway to splash water on his face. It was ice cold, but just the jolt he needed to wake up. He glanced further down the hallway toward Velena's door as he descended the staircase, thinking about the previous night's conversation. Again, he wondered how he'd managed to share with her the way he did, and if he would regret opening up at all.

She'd been gracious in the moment, but surely she'd be laughing at him now. He tried to push his insecurities aside as he reached the lower level of the keep. He wouldn't waste his thoughts on regrets; it took enough concentration just to maneuver past all of the snoring men that lay littered around the Lord's bedchamber. Valets, house servants, the wardrober[10]—it mattered not their station at night, for they all bedded down the same, either on benches or pads scattered round the perimeter of the room. All except his uncle who, as bailiff, occupied the trundle beneath the Baron's large four-poster feather bed.

Stepping over the last snoring body and slipping out the door, Tristan breathed deeply of the cold winter air as he crunched his way across the gravel yard, ignoring the light drizzle, usually referred to as nothing more than *good English weather.*

It had taken him a while to fall asleep last night, but once he did, it was full of dreaming. Tristan walked on toward the barracks. He remembered waking to thoughts of Gwenhavare, but was becoming quickly aware of another dream he'd had even before that. This one was of Velena, but he was having trouble recalling it.

The young esquire shook his head to clear the fog and began his stretches. Satisfied, he jogged past the inner and outer gatehouses, and out over the moat bridge. He set his course, choosing to run around the perimeter of the moat, intent on checking out the woods that lay to the west.

Years of running had made his legs strong and sure footed, so that they carried him over the uneven ground with little effort. His mind began to clear and his dream of Velena began to take shape. She'd been walking beside him, smiling as she spoke. He couldn't hear her voice, but he remembered her excitement. He heard himself promising her something, and then she'd offered him her hand—her words were coming back to him.

Tristan veered from the castle towards the forest, jumping over rocks and watery dips in the ground as he went. His breath became more ragged, but still he ran. *What was it she'd said?* Walk with me. That was it; she'd said, *will you walk with me?* He hadn't had time to respond, for the dream seemed to change after that.

Chest heaving, Tristan stopped short of entering the woods, still running in place until his heart rate slowed. Back to the reality of yesterday, he could see Velena in his mind's eye, on the floor, seated across from him. He remembered watching her face. She hadn't been laughing at him. She'd offered her hand as a sign of friendship, and he'd taken it.

If Velena had been Gwenhavare, he felt certain he would have kissed it, but despite the fact that she wasn't, he realized how in need of human interaction he was, and how lonely he'd been feeling up until the point Velena had accepted him so readily—so sincerely. He passed by the trees at a brisk walk, anxious to pray and anxious to return.

[10] **Wardrober:** Servant in charge of his master's clothing.

good company

The Baron's chamber had been set up for morning business. A long table had been moved center, where Lord Richard and Lord Rolland hunched over the financial expenses for the week.

They were not alone in the large room. Several knights sat on benches polishing their swords and sharpening their knives; the wardrober had the Baron's clothing laid out upon the bed to mend and to cull out various pieces to have laundered; and servants milled about performing sundry tasks such as replacing the rushes on the floor and the hay for toilet uses in the garderobe.[11] On the other end of the table, Velena and Tristan sat silently over a game of chess.

"Check," Velena knocked Tristan's pawn out of place with gusto.

Tristan gave her a cocky look, "Check mate," he said, raising one eyebrow.

"What? I didn't see your castle there. You cheated!" Velena's voice rose, causing heads to turn in their direction.

Lords Richard and Rolland exchanged smiles as the knights winked at one other and chuckled at the pair of them. It'd been more than five months since Tristan had visited Velena's solar, and their argumentative banter was quickly becoming the new normal around the castle.

"Because you didn't see it, I cheated?"

"Exactly so," Velena said lowering her voice, "You distracted me with your finger tapping."

"I doubt it."

"Yes. I haven't been able to concentrate since we started. You should have warned me about your castle; it would have been the *esquirely* thing to do."

"I see."

"Good."

"Wait! What are you doing?"

"Putting my king back."

"What? No." Tristan quickly reached across the board, plucking it from her hand.

"You said, *I see.*"

"I meant that I understood!"

Lord Rolland raised an eyebrow of warning to his nephew. "Keep it down to a low roar if you don't mind."

Velena crossed her arms and leaned forward on the table, "You know it's very frustrating not to be able to understand you plainly.

"Noted. But that doesn't change the fact that I'm not taking back my move."

"Well, it should. You understood that I was distracted and could see that I didn't see your castle. If I had, I wouldn't have chosen to put your king in check since…"

"That doesn't even begin to make sense."

"I'm making a clearly stated argument. You know, it's equally as frustrating when you don't understand me."

Tristan pulled at his hair. "It upsets you when you don't understand me, and it upsets you when I don't understand you. So you get to vent your frustration either way, is that it?"

Velena straightened her posture as she stared over at him smugly. "I'm well aware of my double standards, sir. Now put my king back!"

"Not even if you said please."

Sir Richard thumped the table, "Enough! How can a man think with the two of you around? Take it outside."

Laughter, clapping, and a smattering of, "Here, here!" followed them out the door, neither person the least bit daunted by the heckling.

"You still cheated."

"I..."

"Did."

"Not!"

"Mean to cheat—yes, I know. So I forgive you."

Tristan chose a direction at random and started walking. "Velena."

"Yes."

"You lost."

"Fine," she said rolling her eyes. "We'll just have to play again."

"Why would you want to play a cheat?"

"But you didn't mean to cheat."

"Are you sure?"

"I can tell an unintentional cheater from an intentional one."

Tristan laughed outright and stopped, "How is it that you're always so...?"

"Delightful?" Velena finished, his sentence sauntering off ahead of him, hands held behind her back, flashing her very best smile from over her shoulder.

Tristan laughed again as he stared after her, wondering if she knew how the swinging of her hips affected a person. He followed. "This was you being delightful?"

"Well, sometimes I can be competitive and pushy," she whispered, leaning in towards him, "but you haven't seen that side of me yet."

"Still? Are there any warning signs?"

"None at all." They both came to a halt.

"Hm. Well then, I think I'd better retire to my solar and rest up for our next match; I suddenly feel very fatigued."

"You do not, and we just got here."

"Your lady's maid can keep you company."

"Daisy? Where?"

"Over yonder," Tristan gestured with his head.

Daisy was standing with Jonas and Kat out by the corral watching Bowan exercise Sir Fredrick's horse.

"She's smitten."

"Most assuredly," Tristan agreed, grinning down at Velena, "but as for me, as delightful as your company is—and it is—I have some reading I've been looking forward to doing."

"That book your friar friend gave you?"

"Mm-hm. Will you be okay, here?"

"Yes, I'll join Daisy. She'll admire the squire, and I'll—"

"Admire the horse."

"Velena giggled, "Chat with Jonas and Kat. You're awful; go read your book."

Smiling from ear to ear, Tristan gave an exaggerated bow before turning his feet back towards the keep. Ever since the day he'd visited her solar, life had changed for them. The heavy veil of mourning had finally been lifted, and pain had made room for small pleasures as they walked in the newness of their friendship, receiving from it the blessings of happiness to replace the days they'd lost to depression.

---

[11] **Garderobe:** A small chamber where the toilet is located.

a man of character

Sir Richard had just returned to the keep from making his circuit around the inner bailey, when he looked up to see Velena and Daisy walking across the yard.

"Velena." Sir Richard raised his arm and motioned for her to join him, noticing that Tristan was not with her, for once. He knew it wasn't the wisest relationship for him to encourage, but he couldn't bring himself to find fault with it—not after having watched his daughter fall deeper and deeper into an abyss, helpless to reach her. Yet in only a few short weeks of his arriving, Tristan had been able to accomplish what he could not, and for that, Richard would be forever grateful.

Velena approached. She was in cheerful disposition. "Yes, Father?"

"Walk with me, my girl; it's been a while since we've talked."

Daisy hesitated to follow. "Shall I allow you your privacy, my lord?"

"No, no. You're welcome to come along. I hate to be indoors when there is such fine weather to be had. So where is Tristan today?"

"He's reading."

"That's good to hear. A reading man is an intelligent man; I see that in him. Tell me, what is his book of choice?"

Velena's forehead wrinkled. "I don't really know. I've always just assumed it was something of a religious nature; it was a friar that gifted it to him. I think he must love reading as I do. I regret we weren't able to bring more books with us from our library at Landerhill."

"I'll see if Rolland has any books tucked away someplace that you might get your hands on, but in the meantime it's good you've found someone with whom you have so much in common."

"You approve of our time together?"

"You still know your place, I assume?"

"With Peter, Father."

"Good girl." Sir Richard looked at his daughter with open affection. "As long as you remember your obligations, I'll not separate you from a companion of your own age and station. We're poor for company, and I'm not oblivious to the monotony that this place affords. I feel it myself."

"Have you been missing Mother?"

"Very much."

"And Britton?"

Her father didn't answer at the mention of his only son, but raised both hands to his lips as if praying.

"Why hasn't he written? Surely, Wolf or Sir Tarek would have forwarded a letter to us if he had."

"These are dangerous times for traveling, Velena. I'm not sure we'll know anything anytime soon, and every day that goes by is another day I fear for his safety. The arms of this wretched Pestilence are far reaching."

Daisy shook her head as if to signify what a pity his situation was. "There used to be no better place in all the world than England."

"The French would disagree with you. King Edward certainly has his work cut out for him, trying to fight a war and a Plague at the same time. Death is no respecter of persons, though—not in peace and definitely not in war. The nobility on both sides will certainly feel its sting before long, if it hasn't already."

"Will they stop the fighting and negotiate, then?" Daisy looked hopeful.

"I couldn't say for certain, but I doubt it. France will never accept Edward's claim to their throne, and Edward will have his land."

Velena hated the idea of men still having to kill each other when the Plague was doing such a good job of it all by itself. "What will he do?"

"Edward has his faults as a man, but he's a good king—despite the pathetic influence he had in his father. He'll do what's best for England. I may be called away to court and then we'll have some proper news. Until then we're a bit in the dark."

Velena's heart sank, and she pulled on her father's arm to stop, "You won't go, will you?!"

"I won't have a choice, my girl, nor would I want one. Things are happening in England and we mustn't be ignorant of them. Surely, you know that?"

"Yes, Father." She said it with words, but not with her heart. Focusing on the rest of the conversation now became a challenge.

"Cheer up, Daughter, that could still be some time away. Besides, Tristan makes for a hardy distraction, and he'll be able to help his uncle with the castle in my absence.

"I'm glad you approve of his character, Father?"

"I do, yes. There's been nothing to disapprove of that I've taken note of, unless a man can be judged by the cut of his hair."

Daisy giggled, "He needs his own valet."

"A very astute observation, Daisy; I've been meaning to bring that up to Rolland. Esquire that he is, he ought to have one and would have probably arrived with one, if he hadn't had to make the journey here as he did. I've overlooked his needs."

"I don't think he'd care for one," Velena said.

"Who is he esquire to?" asked Daisy.

"His father was Sir Tobias Challener, a knight of no meager means. He made a career of the tournament circuit and a real killing doing it. He acquired no small fortune and left his wife more than comfortable when he died."

Daisy's eyes were wide with curiosity. "Was it a tragic death? I'll bet his wife never recovered from it."

"I'm sure it was to his family—good heavens, what sorts of books have you been giving this girl to read, Velena?" he said, chuckling at the overly dramatic, now frowning, Daisy.

"I only have *Tristan and Isulte* with me, Father."

"Well, we can't be filling a head as pretty as yours with only romance." He chided Daisy directly. "We'll have to get you something on philosophy or religion. Perhaps Tristan will lend you his."

"I'll ask him, my lord," Daisy said, having no intention of doing so.

"But to answer your question, no; it was no glorious death on the field of battle, if that's what you were hoping for. He died after eating some spoiled meat, I believe. And although considerably distraught, his wife did, in fact, carry on, Daisy—as most women do. It is the husbands who waste away without their wives."

"Not in your case, my lord."

"That's because Father is an exceptional man," Velena said with a wink.

"Alright, what is it you want? Name it and it's yours," he said with a laugh.

"Only you, Father. Promise me you won't waste away to nothing. We couldn't do without you."

"Poor Tristan." Daisy sighed. "He has no one, now that his mother and sisters are gone."

"He has Lord Rolland," Velena corrected.

"And an elder brother besides," Lord Richard added. Now that his mother's gone, Tristan is master of her home in Oxford. He won't be receiving the lion's share of the inheritance, but he'll be in no way destitute."

Velena kicked at a rock laying in her path, "I never thought of Tristan as a rich man."

"When he gets back into town, he'll be an esquire of esquires, no doubt, gaining the attentions of many a young widow, all of them left rich, themselves, from their husband's deaths—only adding to his wealth. His land and holdings will put him in a very affluent position.

His time at the Studium Generale will also be to his favor—nothing worse than a stupid man of wealth. I wonder that his marriage wasn't arranged for before his mother died."

"He's never mentioned it." This was a new thought for Velena. "Will you put his educational talents to good use while he's here?"

"I will, indeed. I've already asked Rolland to take him on as his treasurer. According to him, he's exceptionally good with numbers, and quite frankly, after the great headache we've had today over doing it ourselves, I'll be happy to hand it over to someone else. Rolland hasn't had a descent treasurer since Thomas died last year, and it's just too much for him to take on with all his other responsibilities."

"I'm pleased you can trust him with such things."

"I trust him with you, don't I?"

Velena laughed. "Don't worry Father, I can't imagine falling in love with him."

"And I'll hold him personally responsible if that changes."

"Do you think as highly of Peter as you do of Tristan?"

"Well that's a question isn't it? And there's no simple answer for it. Your uncle is as unpleasant a man as ever there was one, and taken on his own, I couldn't believe him capable of raising a man worth his salt, but he married your mother's closest friend, the Lady Madeline, and there was a good woman. Whatever goodly character traits Peter received, he receives from her. Even more to his benefit would be the time he's spent growing up with his mother's family, serving under a most worthy knight until knighted himself. His visits were always pleasant, to which I think you would concur, and in addition to all this, he was a favorite of your mother's, being her first nephew and the son of her friend. I've no doubt he'll manage his father's estate well when the day comes. He's handsome enough to please any woman, well-mannered and educated—but more than that, it's what your mother wanted. I'm confident you'll be happy in your situation—if you can manage to avoid your uncle."

Both girls laughed. "Have you always been at odds with Uncle Magnus?" Velena inquired.

Sir Richard paused before answering. "Daisy, now would be a good time for you to catch up on something that needs done."

"Yes, my lord," Daisy said, walking away disappointed that she wouldn't be present for this intriguing bit of information.

Sir Richard guided his daughter to the fishing pond in the outer bailey where they seated themselves on carved stone benches.

"You never knew your grandfather because he was a sickly man and died shortly after your mother and I were engaged. In fact, we'd only had our names put upon the door of the church a week when he passed, God rest his soul. The day after he died, Magnus was there to dispute the marriage. He claimed that Cecilia was already promised to someone else, which was entirely false."

"Why would he say that?"

"He's greedy. He wanted your mother to marry a widower count, who had twice the lands and twice the clout in court that I had. Magnus thinks of no one but himself, and he cared not that the count was twenty years her senior or known for beating his previous wife well beyond what was necessary."

"How then did you come to marry her?"

Sir Richard grinned. "The count was greedy as well. He turned his eye to a widow countess, someone or other, who had a handsome fortune of her own, and so he abandoned Magnus' ambitious desires for him and his sister. In the end, your uncle had to come crawling back, and he never got over the humiliation."

"Did you want to marry Mother?"

"From the very start. She was a lovely girl, sweet tempered and kind—only fourteen when your grandfather promised her to me."

Velena sat quietly next to her father, leaning her head against his strong shoulder. "Do you think Peter wants to marry me?"

"What's not to want? You're the picture of your mother. You have her dark hair and green eyes—beautiful inside and out."

"Do I really remind you of her?"

"Very much."

"Does that bother you?"

"No—no, on the contrary," he said, putting his arm around her shoulders and hugging her close, "It makes life easier for me—knowing a part of her still remains." His eyes were distant, but his smile was sincere. "I know Magnus will come for you eventually, but I'm not looking forward to giving you up just yet, especially not knowing about your brother."

There was a moment's pause, and then Lord Richard lifted his free hand to pinch the tears off from between his eyes, making no effort to hide his emotion. "You're precious to me, Velena. Don't ever doubt it."

He released his hold on her then so that he could look her in the face. Cecilia looked back. Yes, a part of her still lived on.

"Go on girl, find that book reading friend of yours and let an old man pray in peace."

"You're not old, Father—and Brit's still alive."

"I've prayed for little else. Perhaps Sir Makaias will send word if Britton can't."

"Who?"

"Sir Makaias is eldest brother to Sir Andret and Squire Jaren."

"Oh yes, the serious one."

Sir Richard chuckled. "Perhaps. But if you want to talk about a man of character, you couldn't leave him out of the conversation. There was a time I was hoping he'd be a good match for you, but he had no fortune, and your mother was set on Peter."

Velena scrunched up her face at the distasteful idea. "He barely spoke two words to me the last time he visited Landerhill. I don't think he liked me."

Sir Richard grinned. "His loss."

"There's simply no possible way for me to stay near you and remain a humble human being," Velena announced, popping up from the bench with a laugh, "I'll let you get to your prayers."

She kissed her father's cheek and he sat watching her trot off as if she hadn't a care in the world—if only he could return her to the days when that was true.

the rider

Summer breezes whipped across Velena's face as she and Tristan galloped their horses through the high stone arches of the portcullis, and thundered across the bridge. The wind pulled at her full-skirted tunic and clawed her hair loose from its golden circlet as they sped past open fields. Red poppies and wild flowers of various hues and varieties waved their greeting as their colors shown brilliantly in the morning sun.

Not stopping to admire the finery around them, they raced on to the tree line, kicking up dirt and rocks as they flew over uneven ground. Velena felt as though she'd been given wings, and if she could have made it so, she would have unfurled them now so that they could lift her high above the earth—higher than the fast approaching trees— higher than the clouds.

She knew of no safe place to land, so perhaps she would just go on soaring forever—hovering above all the ugliness of the world, out of reach of the Plague, and, if possible, beyond even the notice of the God who unleashed it.

"Whoa!" Tristan pulled on the reigns, signaling an end to their race and Velena's reverie of taking flight.

They'd reached their destination, and the high-spirited equines tossed their muscular necks and chomped at their bits in disapproval of the slow pace with which they were now compelled to walk.

Tristan reached down and patted Augustine's quivering chestnut shoulder. "That a boy, nice and easy."

He turned to Velena, panting from excitement as though he'd run the distance himself. The wind had blown his sandy brown colored hair even more out of place than normal, but his eyes sparkled and the joy of the moment filled his countenance.

"They certainly have spirit. That was fantastic; truly, we should do this more often."

Velena's demeanor could not have been in greater contrast to his own as she stared uncertainly into the temple of trees before them. Her horse still fought to free its head, but she gripped the reigns with an expert hand, so that she hardly noticed her tantrum. "I don't know, Tristan, I'm still not much for leaving the castle."

"So I've noticed." Tristan watched her with a knowing expression.

When he wasn't in his room reading, or about the business of Lord Richard, Tristan spent most of his waking moments with Velena, and although they'd not talked much of intimately personal subjects, he was observant by nature and knew when she was feeling more than what she was saying. He wanted her to open up to him, but the constant restless movements of the horses did not provide the calming atmosphere he was hoping for.

"Let's walk," he said, hoping for the right moment to present itself.

They dismounted and began leading their horses into the enchanted world of living pillars, each one towering above them ripe with green. Despite its summer beauty, Velena couldn't help remembering winter, and the way the branches looked upon their first arrival—all fanned out in a great many gnarled hands, all reaching heavenward, in their attempt to beg God for mercy. How dare their leaves spring forth now, unsympathetic to the dying world around them. Did they now flourish on the blood of men?

Tristan interrupted her thoughts. "Talk to me, Velena. What's weighing on you?"

She didn't hesitate. "Do you think we'll live through this? Will secluding ourselves really keep us safe?"

Tristan's thoughts were confirmed. "If God wills it. He's still sovereign."

"Sovereign." Velena said the word as though trying it on for the first time, only to find it was a wrong fit. "Do you think He meant to take my mother—and yours, to…to take them, and others, and to leave us behind?"

"Do you?" he said, feeling it wise to redirect her question.

Velena took the bait and chewed on it a while, trying to make sense of her own thoughts. "I don't know. Why would He? I mean, if He's an all wise, all knowing God, then He knows the day of our deaths, and, if He knows the day of our death and doesn't stop it, then it's as good as saying that He plans our deaths. So, He took them—on purpose."

Tristan moved the conversation along gingerly. "I would agree. He does have our days numbered, but I think what you're really wrestling with is, is that act an action of good or evil?"

"I'd be a heretic to say that God was evil." It was not a question, but somewhere between voice and thought, Tristan heard it all the same. "His ways are supposed to be good—by virtue of them being his ways, which is…is a whole other thought to ponder," she muttered. Velena waved her hand and shut her eyes tight as if to cut the rabbit trail out of her thinking. "So, if in His essence He is good, then when he ended their lives He was either being gracious to them by allowing them to escape this hell on earth, or to us by allowing us to live through it, and…"

"And what?" Tristan asked, afraid he'd say too much and shut her down. She'd never opened up this way before, and he knew she desperately needed to lay down her burdens.

"And what sort of mercy is that? What's life if it's lived in fear?"

"Are you afraid?"

"Every day." Velena glanced sideways to see his reaction to her words, and there were those eyes staring back at her.

The rustling grass beneath their feet grew quiet as they stopped;

even the horses stood still as if understanding the gravity of the moment.

Tristan approached Velena until they were only inches apart. Her hair was disheveled, but charmingly so to Tristan's mind; he watched dark strands blow across her face, creating lines of vision leading to high cheek bones, a pleasant mouth, and resplendent green eyes dressed in a golden circlet of their own.

He thought again how attractive she was, but it wasn't the color of her hair or her eyes that drew his attention, but rather the mask she'd just pulled away. To him she'd been witty and pleasant, intelligent and fun—but not vulnerable. He wanted to put his arms around her, but touching was not their way.

Velena stiffened at his closeness, but didn't step away. She wondered what he was thinking as his eyes roved over her face, admiring her features and embracing her pain. She waited for him to speak, but he said nothing. "Why are you staring at me?"

"I didn't know."

"That I was afraid?"

"How much it consumed you; I wish I'd known."

"You couldn't have."

Tristan took the reins from Velena's hands and left her staring after him as he tethered Augustine and Guinevere to the closest tree.

"Let's sit." He gestured for her to join him in the grass, and then laughed as she held her hands behind her back, sashaying her way over to him in slow exaggerated movements. She spread out her navy skirts like royalty about her feet.

"As you wish."

"Are you trying to distract me from the subject at hand?"

"I may be trying to lighten the mood. I don't need to be disposing my burdens on you. I'm sorry."

"Sorry for…Velena, that's what we're here for; it's why…why we exist—to bear one another's burdens, to hold each other up. Jesus says to love each other as ourselves; do you think I could march forward to sanity without looking behind me to notice that you're faltering?"

Velena picked at the grass and flicked at a passing scarlet colored beetle, her mouth turned down at the corners. "I really thought I was doing better. Tristan, you've lost so much more than I have. How are you not afraid?"

Tristan slouched back on his palms, "I think that fear is an awful thing, and I'd rather not spend any more time in its presence than I have to."

Velena's heart sunk; she really thought he might have the answers she needed, but then he continued.

"Sometimes I'm afraid, but honestly, Velena, God gives us promises that help us escape from that place of fear."

"What promises?"

Friar Daniel once read something to me from the Holy Scriptures, a psalm written by King David. It says, *"The Lord is my light and my salvation; whom shall I fear? The Lord is the defense of my life; whom shall I dread? When evildoers came upon me to devour my flesh, my adversaries and my enemies, they stumbled and fell. Though a host encamps against me, my heart will not fear; though war arises against me, in spite of this I shall be confident. One thing I have asked from the Lord, that I shall seek: that I may dwell in the house of the Lord all the days of my life, to behold the beauty of the Lord and to meditate in His temple. For in the day of trouble He will conceal me in His tabernacle; in the secret place of His tent He will hide me; He will lift me up on a rock."*

Velena was distractedly tossing pieces of broken grass into his cupped hands while he recited from memory. He wasn't sure how well she was listening, but he continued on until the end. *"I would have despaired unless I had believed that I would see the goodness of the Lord in the land of the living. Wait for the Lord; be strong and let your heart take courage; yes, wait for the Lord."*

Velena looked up then, "My mother believed that God was good," she finally said.

"He is. Think of what he did for Israel...*and the Lord heard our voice and saw our affliction and our toil and our oppression; and the Lord brought us out of Egypt with a mighty hand and an outstretched arm."*

"Do you think that existing beneath these same arms, today, qualifies us for this same mercy? Does He see *our* affliction?"

"I do—and yes, He does."

"Hm." Velena grasped his wrist, tipping his hand over to watch the blades of grass fall into his lap.

"No one would argue with you that it's difficult to be left behind when those we love are not with us anymore."

"Harder still when you don't know if they're dead or alive."

"Your brother?"

"….and Peter."

"Your intended?"

"I was to be married by the time I turned sixteen; then came this Pestilence. Well, that's come and gone. His family wouldn't come with us because my uncle had *affairs* to attend to—which is ridiculous. As if one's affairs matter if everyone is dead!"

Tristan chose to ignore the morbid picture she was bent on painting, and chuckled instead at the idea of her getting married, "Poor sap. If he ever makes it over this way, I'll warn him not to beat you at chess."

"Warn him not to cheat."

"That too." Tristan tossed the pile of grass at her face and then smiled to himself, embarrassed by his thoughts."

"What's so funny?"

"We're kind of in our own little world over here. Certain things, like you getting married, just don't cross my mind."

"Oh, well, what about you? You've never mentioned if you were engaged?"

"I am not, as a matter of fact. My match was not made for me. When my father died, my mother was left to live quite comfortably in the wealth he'd left behind. When I was nine she sat me down and said, 'Son, I'm going to give you a gift and it's one you get to choose for yourself. When you become a man, you shall marry for love.'"

"Really?"

"Really. She loved my father and wanted me to have the same. Though as you grow up and realize that most women are engaged by the time they're two, you find that the pickings are rather slim. I suppose it's the thought that counts." Tristan chuckled.

"So you never found anyone?"

"There was one woman, but…"

"But what?"

"It wasn't meant to be."

"What's her name?"

Tristan ducked his head in embarrassment. "No, it's past now."

"Come on. Tell me about her."

"It doesn't matter anymore." Tristan pushed himself up to standing, boyishly grinning in a way Velena had never seen before. His face lit up like a smoldering coal receiving new oxygen, and its heat was aflame all over his face

"You're turning red—now you have to confess. Tell me about her or I'll whine."

Tristan tried forcing himself not to smile, but he couldn't. "Alright, but don't make sport of it."

"Me?"

Tristan rolled his eyes. "I was studying at the Studium Generale in Oxford. I rarely made time for parties or social gatherings, in fact, I hated them and tried to spare myself the experience as much as possible, but my mother was going to one and insisted that I accompany her and my sisters."

Tristan grew quiet for a moment at the mention of his family, but quickly continued, pressing through the emotion. "Anyway, there was this girl there, different from anyone else."

"Was she pretty?"

"Beautiful. I worked up the courage to dance with her and then we sat and talked for the rest of the night. She had me completely bewitched. I still dream about her sometimes—it keeps her face clear in my mind."

"Oh, Tristan."

"After that, I rarely caught more than a glimpse of her at church, but I...I couldn't get her out of my head; I had a difficult time focusing on my studies after that. The trivium only meant as much to me as I could apply it to her, and I wanted to know everything about her."

"Did you speak again?"

"Not really."

"What?!"

"I...I wouldn't know what to say when I did see her, so I usually never got past the hellos. The last time I saw her was when I left the friar at Oxfordshire."

Velena untangled her legs from her gown and rose to stand with him. "She's your *Isulte*."

"My what?"

"Your *Isulte*. You know, the story of *Tristan and Isulte*."

"I know the story, but I don't see the connection other than my name. Though I wouldn't mind her being my *Isulte*; does Daisy carry around any extra love potions with her that I could borrow?"

"She doesn't love you back?"

"I don't think I'll ever get the chance to find out."

"She must love you, Tristan. Wait and see. I hope for your sake God is good, as you say, and perhaps then you'll live to see your *Isulte* return your love. Maybe too, Peter will live and we'll get married as well."

"Do you love Peter?"

"Not as you love. We were betrothed as children; I wasn't as fortunate as you."

"No, you were more so. Gwe..."

"*Isulte*," Velena corrected him, "Have faith."

"*Isulte* was most likely promised to another. One man's freedom to choose does not benefit him more than the woman who has security in a man chosen for her—or something like that."

"But you're free to love whomever you wish, and you love her; it seems too unfair that she could belong to another."

"I like the way you think," he said and laughed out loud, "But what of you? You're still free to love."

"You mock my lack of choice, do you?" she said wryly.

"Love is a choice, Velena. You could choose to love Peter."

"I'm not sure it's as easy as choosing. Could you do as you suggest?" Velena crossed her arms, giving Tristan a moment to ponder her exact meaning, "Do you think you could choose to love Isulte of the *White Hands* if you couldn't have the Isulte of your dreams?"

"Isulte of the White Hands? I don't remember reading about her."

"She was the Isulte that Tristan married, but wouldn't bed, because the Isulte he loved was married to the king. He could have chosen to love his new wife, but he wouldn't because he longed for the first Isulte."

Tristan laughed. "Exactly how far are we taking this book analogy?"

"Just answer the question."

Tristan smiled but chose his words cautiously. "I think that I'll *not* think on that till I must," he said, sensing his own reluctance to go down that road.

"Do you know what I think?"

"What?"

"I think your Isulte is a very fortunate woman."

Tristan accepted her compliment. "So is your intended— despite your double standards," he said, delightfully satisfied as her hands jumped to rest upon her hips.

"Is that supposed to be a compliment?"

"Very much so."

Velena felt the sincerity of his praise, despite his jest, and smiled. "Come on, we should…"

"Shh. Did you see that?"

"See what?

"Back where we came—out past the trees." Tristan and Velena jogged back over to their horses. He gave Velena a leg up before mounting his own.

"What was it?"

"I only saw a shadow, but it looked like a horse."

Velena felt the blood rush from her temples as she clucked Guinevere forward towards home. They trotted the horses the short distance back to the tree line and looked toward the castle.

"There." Tristan pointed as he took site of a horse and rider making the turn onto the moat bridge. "Come on, maybe there's news."

"Tristan, wait..." but her objection came too late.

He'd already raced ahead, and she had little choice but to follow. Guinevere was already trembling in anticipation of what she thought was going to be a merry chase.

one step forward

"Ouch!" Velena said as she slapped at Daisy's hand.

"Sorry, my lady, but your hair is knotted in every direction; I'm trying to be gentle." Daisy began again, working the silver brush through her mistress's waste length hair.

Meanwhile, Velena fingered the un-ornamented golden circlet in her lap, satisfied with the way the smooth metal felt in her hands. It gave her something to focus on, which was helpful because she was still upset that she'd been unable to speak with her father about the rider.

The stranger had been led into the great hall, but couldn't have been there more than fifteen minutes before her father and Lord Rolland left with him at their heels. They were holding manorial court outside the castle walls.

Velena felt much the same as her horse had earlier, her mind was also racing at neck breaking speeds wondering what on earth that man was here for, and now she was chomping at the bit because there was no more road. Not only did she wonder why he was here, but she couldn't help but fear for what he might have brought with him. Was the Plague still running rampant in the world or had the butcher finally put down its knife?

"Daisy?"

"Yes, my lady."

"I don't want you near the rider that came today until we find out where he's come from—just in case."

"In case he brings the Plague, I know. Don't worry about me; you couldn't force me near the man. Plague or no, he smells to high Heaven, and that's the truth. I heard from Bowan that he was given food in the hall and his manners were atrocious. I don't know what possible news he could bring that's worth hearing. I'd wager he's no messenger at all, probably just some vagrant needing lodging for the night."

"If that were so, he'd be lodged outside the castle walls. I don't think he'd have gotten past the gate unless he had some sort of news." Restless, Velena slapped the circlet down on the table making a loud clinking sound. "Are you almost finished?"

"You can feel your hair is down and undone the same as I can see it." Daisy dimpled. "How would you like it arranged?"

"A plait is fine."

Daisy was half way through the twists and turns of the thick plait when the distant noise of men shouting drifted up through her window.

"What on earth...? Follow me." Velena's chair scraped back on the floor as she rushed over to the window with Daisy trailing behind her trying to salvage the tail end of her efforts. "I can't see anything from here. It must be coming from the green."

"Your father's holding court—maybe there's a fight."

"Tristan's there."

Daisy raised her eyebrows. "So is his uncle, your father and a dozen others; I'm sure he's fine."

Velena knit her brow in concern. She did *not* want to go out there—so many people. But Tristan was there, and if something was amiss, she didn't want to be left in the dark, like she was about the rider. "Let's go and make sure."

"My lady, what could we do even if he wasn't? And you hate going out of the castle." Daisy finished securing Velena's hair, just as she pulled away and went for the hallway.

"I was just out for a ride, wasn't I?"

"And you hated it."

"I want to know, that's all."

Daisy clucked her tongue. "I don't know what your father's going to say when he finds out."

Velena was almost half way down the stairs. "Finds out what?"

"About you and Tristan," she hissed, "you're so obvious about it. You're going to end up with a broken heart, and it breaks mine to think of it."

Velena stopped short, turning to see if Daisy was in earnest. She was. "Daisy, what on earth do you mean? There's nothing about me and Tristan that my father should need to know."

"Are you denying you're in love with him? And to me of all people!" Daisy looked aghast and came to stand on the step next to her, keeping her voice to a whisper. "I've never given you cause to doubt my loyalty; I wouldn't breath it to a soul, but it's getting to the point where I won't have to."

Velena could have denied the allegation right away, but was so taken aback that her failure to answer served only to justify Daisy's claim. "I've kept nothing from you."

Daisy's confusion was apparent, "I'm sorry, but how could you think that no one else has taken note of the way that you and Tristan…"

"There's nothing to take note of!" Velena's voice echoed in the stairwell, raising several heads in the chamber below.

Back to whispering. "Really, Daisy, you insult my honor to even suggest it. There's nothing between Tristan and I that would stand in the way of my marriage to Peter. I've not failed to include you in my confidences because there's nothing to confide—so no self-pity, please. Go back upstairs and fetch a blanket for us to sit on."

"I just don't want to see you hurt."

"The blanket—and feel free to take your time." By now, Velena's voice was harsh, as she turned, stomping her way down the empty staircase.

Daisy threw back the bedroom door. Did Velena truly think that she didn't have eyes in her head? Daisy knew she couldn't just be seeing things that weren't there. *How can she reasonably expect me to believe that she is not in love with Tristan? Ridiculous!*

Blanket now in hand, Daisy's lightweight tunic dragged along rushes and herbs, no longer sweet smelling, as she rustled past the men loitering in the lower room. Why should it even matter to her? It was Velena's future that was in jeopardy, not her own. Except that Velena was lying to her, and Velena never lied to her. It didn't make any sense, unless…unless Velena didn't even recognize it herself—how tragic! It was perfectly obvious to Daisy that Tristan was wooing her, and right under the very nose of her father; she had only assumed Velena had responded in kind. She was now beginning to think that this could all be Tristan's fault. Velena was an innocent, blind to the evils of men.

Daisy never gave the slightest thought to the fact that she, too, was an innocent, and one with an overly active imagination at that. Well, the sooner that Velena realized that Tristan was in love with her, the sooner she could act with more discretion towards him, for there was no way that Tristan could ever be considered as a replacement for Peter. Velena may not realize what's going on, but Daisy did, and she felt it her duty to protect Velena from herself—and from him.

Meanwhile, Velena had gotten only as far as the inner gatehouse before thinking that she might turn back. *What if someone from the village is sick?* She knew that if she heard even one person cough, it might be enough to throw her into hysterics. What were those words that Tristan had said, *though a host encamp against me, my heart will not fear.* Second gatehouse just ahead. Sir Fredrick stood watch.

"Good day, my lady."

"And to you, Sir Fredrick."

Velena, stood fast, not moving through the archway.

"Might I be of service to you in some way, Lady Velena?"

"No. Thank you, though. I was just thinking of joining my father for court."

"Ahh, well let me secure you an escort," Sir Andret was just then plodding back over the bridge towards them. "Perfect. Sir Andret," he called. "Would you be so good as to retrace your steps so that the Lady Velena could be joined with her father?"

Andret smiled down at her. "A little more exercise is always good for me."

Velena thanked Sir Fredrick and stepped out from beneath the portcullis, joining Andret back out upon the bridge. Velena took a breath, trying to slow the thumping of her heart to match pace with the thudding of Andret's leather shoes upon the wooden planks.

Velena glanced over at the knight, admiring the almond shaped blue eyes set in a handsomely chiseled face, thinking it too bad he was such a quiet man by nature. Though it was, perhaps, only for her own sake that she thought this, for never knowing what the man was thinking had a tendency of making her a trifle uncomfortable. Velena rarely got more than a few sentences out of him at a time. She knew that if she wanted information, she'd have to choose her words wisely. She'd get right to the point.

"Sir Andret, do you know if the stranger that arrived today brought any news of my brother?"

Andret didn't look at her but kept his eyes on the road, skirting grooves and ruts that might cause Velena to trip or stumble. "I've heard no mention of Sir Britton."

"Where you in the hall when my father received the horseman?"

"Yes, my lady, I was."

"What did he say?"

"He presented your father with a letter. I don't know what it said."

"Will the horseman be staying within the castle walls?"

"I don't believe so."

Velena bit her lip in frustration. She was getting nowhere, and knew full well, she'd received her full quota of words from the man, and none of them so far being helpful.

But she put on a pleasant face and thanked him just the same, adding, "If the letter contains any news of Brit, perhaps we'll be able to infer something of your brother as well. If it says anything about Sir

Makaias, I'll let you know straight away."

Sir Andret looked over in surprise, "I'd be indebted to you."

They walked the rest of the way in an awkward sort of silence, drawing ever closer to a sizable and varied group of people scattered across the lawn like wild flowers dotting the landscape. Off to the side, was a long wooden table set up underneath an old oak tree. Seated there was her father, along with Lord Rolland, several record keepers—and Tristan. He was all right; thank God! Velena breathed a sigh of relief.

As they drew closer, Tristan caught sight of her and began looking from her to the crowd, surprised to see her so close to the locals. He whispered something to her father and then got up from the bench to meet her where she stood.

"Velena? What are you doing here?"

"I heard men yelling from my window. I wanted to make sure you…everyone was all right. Who was shouting?"

Sir Andret frowned, directing his comment to Tristan. "This is ugly business; you ought not to fill her head with it."

"Quite so," Tristan said with a nod, "Thank you for seeing the lady to her father."

Andret made a slight bow of his head before excusing himself, assuming rightly that Tristan would completely disregard his advice the moment his back was turned.

"You're going to tell me, aren't you?" Velena asked incredulously.

"Of course I am."

"Can I just say how much I love that you don't treat me like a child?"

"You can. Now look over there at those two fine gentlemen."

"Do you mean the ones locked in the pillory?"

"The very same; they were the cause of the fine sounding disturbance you heard. They were arguing over that young woman over there."

"The one crying?"

"Her husband died last month…"

Velena's took a step back and her hand flew to her mouth before she could help it."

"…of a leg injury," Tristan quickly assured her, looking on with pity, knowing what she thought he was going to say.

"I'm trying," she apologized.

"I can see that you are! You came out here on your own. Bravo, and I mean that."

Velena waved him off with an embarrassed smile. "Stop it! Continue with your narrative: the husband died, and now what about the woman?"

"Well, your father is now losing money on his fief because it's not being worked, so she's been given two more weeks to pick the *man of her dreams* or she'll have to pay a weekly fine until she does."

"And those two men were fighting over her?"

"Just so."

"And which of them is the man she cries for?"

"Neither. According to her, she hates them both. I like to assume she's crying because she's a woman and that's what women do when they get upset."

"Well there's some faulty logic. I'm a woman and am upset with you on a regular basis, yet you've not seen me weep in such a fashion. I believe you may have to rethink the correctness of your theory, sir."

"But who can think with all this crying?"

"Don't be so heartless to her condition."

"On the contrary; her condition makes me all the more thankful for my own."

Velena rolled her eyes, but could not mock his statement. It was a pathetically sad situation, but unfortunately an all too common one. Velena couldn't help putting herself into this poor woman's shoes, hardly able to blame her for her tears. Not only had her husband died, but the two men she now had to choose from were bound head and hands in the pillory, continuing to make bigger asses of themselves as they hurled insults at each other, seemingly oblivious to the humiliation thrusting itself upon them. Having either of these two for a mate would make Velena want to cry too. She was, all at once, very thankful for Peter.

"I have to get back to the table. Will you join us?" Tristan's question broke through her thoughts.

"No, thank you. I braved my fears to see that all was well with you, but I don't think I'm quite ready yet to join you in such a crowd of people."

"You came for me?"

Velena felt the heat rise to her face as she remembered Daisy's earlier accusations. "And to find out what was in the letter, of course."

"Well, worry not, I'll tell you as soon as I hear something. Look." Tristan gestured that she should turn around. Daisy had since arrived and laid out a blanket a good distance back from the table, under the shade of yet another oak tree. She'd also brought some bread and wine for refreshment.

Tristan smiled, "I'll join you when I can."

an understanding

Velena arrived at the blanket, trying to decide whether or not she was still upset about what Daisy had said earlier.

"Did you find out what was wrong?" Daisy asked, tearing off a piece of bread from the loaf and handing it to Velena.

Velena nodded, accepting the wastel as she sat. She could see the back of Tristan's head as he bent over his entry book, recording a fine a house servant had to pay for using excessive amounts of profanity.

"I'm sorry we argued before. You caught me off guard. The truth is Daisy, I've not been lying to you, and before today, caring for Tristan in that way has never even crossed my mind."

"How can you spend so much time in the company of one man, clearly enjoying yourself, and not feel for him what is only natural for a woman to feel for a man? Granted, he's no Peter, but he's handsome enough to tempt a girl in a moment of weakness, is he not?"

Velena laughed at the back handed compliment.

Daisy crossed her arms. "I'm serious."

Tristan chose that moment to turn his head back to look at Velena; he was proud of her for making the trek outside alone. It was a small miracle, and he hoped it would continue.

"I've always liked his eyes," Velena stated, cocking her head sideways.

"Please! You act as if you're seeing him for the first time."

"Daisy, that's enough. If you attended to me as much as you're supposed to, you would see that what you're saying is absurd. Your head has been in the clouds ever since setting eyes on Sir Fredrick's nephew and you've found every excuse in the world to be where he is. I know you like him, but don't project your feelings onto me. I'm not free to love just whomever, so it hasn't occurred to me to do so. I'm grateful for the arrangement with my cousin—and have no desire to spoil it."

"Just because *you* feel that way, doesn't mean he does."

"Tristan is also otherwise…engaged."

"He's to be married?"

"No, not exactly, but he loves a woman—and it's not me. He doesn't think of me in that way; I probably remind him of one of his sisters. And if I love him, it's …it's as a brother. You have nothing to be concerned about."

"He's still a man. Even a man in love will misuse another if given the opportunity."

"Tristan wouldn't."

"For both your sakes, I hope he doesn't."

Velena sighed in defeat. "Let's have some of that wine."

Finally giving up their argument, they spent the next hour drinking the diluted mixture and enjoying the summer weather. Velena felt herself relax, no longer afraid to focus her attentions on the sounds around her. In high spirits she listened to the birds chirping, insects buzzing, and the random conversations of the villeins and knights. She even took pleasure in the thudding of rotten fruit and vegetables upon the pillory as children dared one another to run up and pelt the two bound men.

Daisy and Velena grinned in amusement as the crowd laughed and mothers only halfheartedly chased their children away, allowing room for Sir John of Staybrook to release them from their time served.

Manorial court had finally come to a close, so Tristan excused himself from the table to stretch his legs over by the girls.

"Well, you have quite the set up over here. Anything else I can send Daisy off for to make you more comfortable?"

"Only yourself," Velena quipped.

"Oh good," Tristan knelt down on the blanket, comically bobbling his head from side to side. "I'm right here, Daisy, don't get up."

Daisy giggled, "I suppose, I can see why she likes you."

Tristan laid a hand to his chest, "I'm a likable fellow."

Daisy twisted up her lips into a thoughtful smirk, accentuating the dimple on her left side. "It's possible to be too likable you know—to where you cause unsuspecting females to mistakenly fall in love with you. Have you ever had that problem in the past?" she probed.

Tristan, now suddenly on his guard, raised his eyebrows in confusion, unsure where this line of questioning was going to go. "Um, no. I have never been so fortunate as to have that problem."

"So you'd like to have the problem of causing women to fall in love with you?"

"I think most men would, but…" Tristan looked to Velena for help. "What's going on here? I feel like I've just walked into some sort of wily feminine trap. Have I?"

Velena shrugged her shoulders. "You have. But it's not mine."

"Ahh."

"She doesn't want to say so, but Daisy's in love with you."

"What?!" Daisy spat out, "Of all the silly things to say, you're the one falling in love with him."

"Daisy, if you don't drop this I'm going to…"

"To what? I'm free to my opinion."

"Only if you keep it to yourself."

Tristan began to laugh. "As flattering as this conversation is, I find it highly unlikely that I could be so fortunate as to have captured the depth of affection that you both say comes from the other. What's this about?"

"It's about the pair of you, that's what," Daisy said. "Let's just be honest and open about all of this, shall we? You're not being careful. We've spent months here and the two of you are always in each other's company, but someday her betrothed will come back. Velena will marry, your hearts will be broken and I'll have to be the one to clean up the mess and sop up the tears of a forbidden love."

"Forbidden love? What do you give this girl to read?"

Daisy glared at him.

Tristan mussed up his already mussed up hair. "What exactly would you have us do, ignore each other?"

"Wake up to the fact that you love each other—so that you can stop loving each other."

Tristan's mouth hung open. He had no answer for this. He could have contradicted Daisy or put her in her place, but in truth he realized he'd been struggling with this very question. What *did* he feel for Velena? Lines did seem to be getting a bit hazy lately.

"Daisy, would you please excuse us."

"My lady?" she questioned, turning to Velena for permission. She nodded.

Daisy hoisted her skirts and strode off in the direction of the castle, only mildly concerned at how strained this might make her relationship with her mistress, but wholly confident that this was the talk Tristan and Velena needed to have.

"I'm so sorry Tristan, she brought up this whole subject to me just before I left the castle—accusing us of being a part of some sort of secret love affair. I thought we'd sorted it out, but she's gotten her head so full of romance and intrigue she can't see past her own nose.

Tristan's hands hung off the blanket behind him, picking at some grass, his head bowed and his brow knit. "Perhaps, but I think she's right. I think this is a talk that we ought to have."

"What do you mean? It was only this morning that you told me of your Isulte—and I'm promised; what's to talk about?"

"I know, but…but I feel closer to you then any human being I've ever known. That might sound silly to you, but I've always been generally shy of women, and yet I could tell you anything—and would, if you asked. I care about you and…and I think about you all the time. I love Isulte, but I hardly know her. You on the other hand, I…I feel like I've known my whole life. It just seems like such a contradiction to say that I love her and not you."

"I always assumed you thought of me as a sister."

"I do—and I don't."

Velena's look was difficult to read, "Are you trying to confess that you...?"

Tristan was beginning to hate this conversation, but still he pressed on, "No. I...I don't think I am."

Tristan adjusted himself closer to Velena so that their conversation wouldn't be overheard. "I mean, I know I'm not allowed to be in love with you, but even if I were, I don't...I don't feel jealous of Peter, so I can only assume that I'm not. In some ways, I feel like I already have you—and I'm not talking about marriage. Is that strange?"

Velena let out the breath she'd been holding, and giggled. "No. I feel the same. Perhaps it's difficult for you to say, but not for me. I love you, Tristan—as a brother, as a friend, as a confidant. I was lost in some sort of darkness before you came. Let's not get confused with the nature of our relationship, let's just love each other. I think that's what we've been doing all along. Only now that we've spoken about it, it can be pure and without confusion—like two sworn brothers. Though not birthed from the same women, we've bonded, but it need not lead to romance.

Tristan beamed. "Despite the gender confusion of your analogy, you've explained it exactly. If that's our definition, then I do, indeed, love you—deeply."

"Except for the marriage part."

"I love you except for the marriage part," Tristan chuckled. "That can be our motto."

"We'll have to keep it to ourselves. I dare say, we'll be a bit misunderstood."

"No more than we already are," Tristan pointed out, borrowing Daisy's abandoned wine glass to make his point, and a toast. "To love."

"Without marriage." Velena giggled.

Tristan laughed, dribbling wine down his chin, as Velena did her best not to spill what remained of her own glass. "That actually sounds a bit immoral," he said, using the back of his hand to wipe his mouth.

"It really does. How about…to friendship?"

Tristan smiled. "To friendship—and short lived mottoes."

the letter

"Velena." Lord Richard's voice interrupted their laughter as he approached from behind.

"Father!" Velena pushed herself up from the blanket and rushed to his side. "I've been waiting to speak with you."

"About this letter business, no doubt."

"Indeed. What does it say?"

The Baron's broad shoulders stooped slightly as he exhaled, rubbing at one of his temples with his maimed hand. Velena thought he looked weary.

"I'll leave you two alone," Tristan said, turning to go.

"You might as well stay, Tristan; it'll save Velena the trouble of telling you later. The letter is from your Uncle Magnus. A good bit of news is that your cousins are still alive."

"Thank God!"

"The rest of his letter gives his reasons for not joining us here."

"He's changed his mind about the wedding." Velena felt weak.

"No, nothing like that," Lord Richard said, dismissing her concerns with a wave of the open letter, still in his hand. "But present circumstances as they are, he feels it's best for him to stay where he is and defend his manor from the possibility of intruders, and if all that he says is…true," he said, shifting his weight from one foot to the other, "I agree that it would be the best course of action for him to take at this time."

"Who do you mean? What intruders?"

Sir Richard looked off into the distance. "There are so many dead, that it's left many homes vacant and unattended. Servants have been abandoning their masters, husband their wives—as well as parents their children."

Velena blinked in disbelief.

"Groups of men, and I suppose woman as well, have been roaming about the countryside taking up residence in these abandoned homes, living licentiously, taking what they want, treating each home as if they owned it—depleting it of every resource."

"And then?"

"And then they move on to the next one."

"I don't…I don't understand. What's wrong with these people? Do you mean to say that they're treating life as some sort of frolic? Aren't they afraid?"

Tristan picked up a stone and flung it against the tree. "Eat, drink, and be merry…for tomorrow we die," he muttered.

"But where are the nobles, the sheriffs—is there no law?"

"What can they do?" Lord Richard asked. "It's been reported that in some towns, up to half its residents have already perished."

Velena gripped herself around the waist, trying to control the trembling in her hands. "And Landerhill? Has it been overrun?"

"According to Magnus, Wolf and Sir Tarek have performed their jobs well, they are still alive, and the manor is secure. Although, there are others in town who have suffered substantial losses, such as…"

"Don't tell me who!" Velena said, interrupting her father. "Please, don't tell me." She was visibly shaken by the news. "I'm sorry, I…I just can't hear anymore."

"I'm sorry to have upset you."

"Don't apologize, Father, it's alright. I'll be alright. I think…I think I should go back to the castle and find Daisy. I know she'll want to know…" her voice trailed off, as she began gathering up the food and wine back into the basket. "I can't possibly fold the blanket with you on it, Tristan. Get off," she said curtly.

Taking no offense, Tristan removed himself, groaning inwardly at of all the progress she'd made only that afternoon—now lost. "I'll carry this," he said, taking up the basket.

Velena's chin began to quiver. "I can manage," she said reaching for the handle.

Richard stepped forward, removing the basket from her grip. He pulled his daughter into his chest with both arms, ignoring her struggles to resist him. "I shouldn't have told you," he crooned, "I shouldn't have told you, forgive me."

Velena shook her head and pulled away, her eyelashes already wet with tears. "I wouldn't have let you not tell me. It's just the way things are, and if...God forbid, it's the way things will always be, I have to get used to standing on my own two feet—just like you said."

And with that, she left them standing under the tree, forgetting both blanket and basket in her effort to get away. Lord Richard looked haggard, remembering his own words, now used against him. She was too old to be shielded from such things, but he was growing less and less confident in her abilities to cope with them.

"Keep an eye on her for me, Tristan," he said stalking off.

Tristan nodded, feeling a great ache in his chest, on behalf of his friend. If he didn't have the Scriptures to turn to...would he be any different than she?

apostate

Learning of the insanity that had overtaken the outside world, had not boded well with Velena. And now, even one year later, despite her resolve to stand, she'd been faltering a little more each day, knowing instinctively, that if she didn't grab a hold of something, and soon, she was destined to fall.

Each morning as Daisy helped dress her into colorfully embroidered tunics and surcoats, Velena would provide her own finishing touches—a brave front and a pretty smile. But Tristan knew better. Every morning he ran, he remembered to pray for his friend, beseeching the Lord on her behalf—pleading for the day that her soul would be brought into the light.

Once again Tristan and Velena found themselves running their horses out from beneath the mighty portcullis, only this time the spirited animals were given their heads. One hoof in front of the other, they thundered past the bridge and out into open fields. Neck and neck they ran, flying past the thicket and into the forest, dodging trees and sending birds from their roosts as the stillness of the moment was broken.

"Whoooa," Velena commanded, reigning in a frothy mouthed Guinevere. "That's enough, girl, whoa now."

Velena sat astride her mare, wiping the perspiration from her brow, smile in place. She was wearing a wide-necked, form-fitted red tunic beneath a dark blue and gold surcoat, open at the sides revealing a low wasted leather belt fastened about her slender seventeen-year-old figure. It was August; the days were growing ever warmer, and Velena wished she'd chosen a lighter weight ensemble to go out riding in.

"What did you want to show me?"

Tristan raised a hand urging her to be patient, all the while sporting a giddy look that made him appear years younger. They pressed forward into a more densely populated area of trees, until they were forced to dismount and walk.

Tristan pushed through the foliage and then spread his arms open wide. "Here it is…"

A rushing brook sat nestled in, what used to be, an undisturbed hiding place. "It's breathtaking."

"Isn't it? I found it yesterday while I was out running."

Velena giggled, "From who?"

"From who what?"

"Who were you running from? I was joking with you. You said you were…oh, never mind, it's ruined."

"I get it. You're a funny girl."

"And you're a patronizing boy."

"Then we're even."

"Why do you run out here and not take up with the other knights where they go?"

"Exercise is only half the reason why I do it. Running clears my head; I can pray better after I've had a good run."

"You pray when you run? How did I not know that about you?"

"I'm a man of many mysteries."

Velena laughed. "How long have you been praying that way?"

"Since a couple of days after I arrived. Right after you got me to leave my room, in fact." Tristan flashed her a smile, "Once again, thank you for that."

"Once again, you're very welcome." She looked around at the serenity before her, wishing she could breathe it all in. She closed her eyes, enjoying the sound of the water as it glided along its serpentine path. Her body swayed to the music of calling birds, rustling leaves, and the beating of her own heart.

Velena suddenly had the urge to pray, herself, but the feeling was so foreign that she opened her eyes with a start and gave her shoulders a little shake as if to right her un-rightable thoughts. "Does it really clear your head?"

"Every time." Tristan said, trying to gauge if he should push her any further.

He'd spent many mornings on his knees before the Lord, agonizing over her spiritual well-being, before finally deciding to bring her here today. He knew she was lost and he wanted only for the right opportunity to share Christ's love with her.

"How do *you* find it easiest to pray?" he asked, hoping she'd be honest with him—honest with herself. He was not to be disappointed.

"I haven't prayed since we left home," Velena confessed. "I know it's terrible to admit that, but I tried once, after that letter came from my uncle last summer, only I couldn't find the words anymore."

Tristan smiled sympathetically. "You need to run with me."

"I don't think so," Velena said with a laugh.

Tristan pumped his eyebrows.

"Wait, are you serious?"

"Very."

"Okay then."

"Okay?"

"Let's do it."

"Alright," he said rubbing his hands together, "so the first thing you need to know is…"

"Ready, steady, go!" Velena was off in a flash, startling the horses, and scattering Tristan's final instructions to the wind.

Racing through the trees; she could hear Tristan's strong and steady stride closing in from behind. Without turning she let out a squeal of delight and hoisted her skirts high, above her knees to keep from tripping. Finally, the pain in her side demanded that she come to a stop. Velena was thoroughly winded, bent over and out of breath—

lungs burning. Tristan came up behind her jogging in place, grinning from ear to ear.

"Good take off, but you might want to pace yourself in the future."

"This…this is not…not fun! It's painful, and I…I think I hate it." Velena now walked in a circle arching her back as her lungs fought through side cramps to drag in the much needed air.

"You say that now, but how's your mind?" he said tapping his forehead with his middle finger.

Velena closed her eyes while Tristan waited patiently, finally shaking her head from side to side. "I still don't have the words. Oh, Tristan, this is silly. Let's go back."

"Wait! Can *I* pray for you then?" Tristan asked, catching her elbow with his hand.

He watched her brow wrinkle, familiar with how she always opposed something new that he suggested before accepting it, or pretty much anything he suggested until it became her idea. But he could tell something was stirring within her, and so he shot up a prayer of thanksgiving when she didn't argue.

"Alright, if it makes you happy—go ahead," she quipped. "You have my full permission to pray to the Blessed Virgin, on my behalf. Ask her to give me peace until such a time as I can make confession. How much back penance do you think I'll have to make up?"

"You can make confession right now," Tristan said, hearing the words of Friar Daniel strong and clear. *I count myself blessed that I can use that wonderful time of intimacy to direct them to God.*

Velena's eyes flew open as she stared at him, bewildered. "We don't have a priest!"

"We don't need one."

"Of course we do." She laughed. "I can't make confession to you; that would be sacrilege."

"Not to me—to Jesus. Confess your sins to Him."

"I can't. Tristan? Isn't that wrong?"

"To confess your sins to God?"

"Without a priest."

"No. You've said many times in the past how you've had doubts about what the priests teach. You'll have to trust me that this is one of those things." Tristan sat cross-legged on the ground. It was a sign for her to join him; it was their posture of intimacy, a time for truth—no jokes.

Velena sat before him, knees almost touching. "Tell me, Velena—please. What have you been needing to confess?"

One blink later, Velena's emerald eyes were glassy, and her lower lip began to quiver. She tried to find her brave smile, but it refused to show. "I'm afraid to tell you."

"Do you want me to leave so you can confess it alone," Tristan said, feeling as though he'd made a gross error in judgment. *Who am I to drag this from her?*

"I'm more afraid to tell God," she said as the first of many tears spilled over her cheeks and slid down her neck. She felt that her body was trembling, and she knew why. She knew that no amount of penance in the world would atone for what she confessed next—today, she would fall. "I've lost faith, Tristan. Almost two years we've been here—in prison. I don't believe that God is good anymore. I think He must hate us all. The world's full of death; we're trapped, and there's no escaping it! He's picking us off one by one; why doesn't He just crush our hearts and be done with it?! Why all the pain?"

Velena inhaled, finding it hard to speak. "I used to wish that I could find King David's shelter, God's tabernacle, the...the rock that he would rest me upon. Where are His outstretched arms? Where is his mercy?! I can't find it, and...and even if I could, He wouldn't embrace me now—not when I hate Him so." Her voice crescendoed. "I'm angry at Him, can you understand that?! God, I'm so angry—and tired. I'm so tired."

Velena cradled her knees and rested her cheek upon them, as though she'd reached the end of what strength was allowed her, looking weary in a way Tristan had never seen her before. "I still don't sleep at night," she continued. "I just lay awake, worrying that tomorrow morning someone will scream out that the Plague has come for us again. Everyone I love is here…my father, Daisy—you. Even your uncle is so kind. What would I do? I keep wondering if I'd run away or stay and tend to you until everyone's corpses finally surround me, leaving me to die alone."

Tristan tried not to react to the bluntness of her words, but she saw it, however subtle.

"I thought you'd gotten past the nights."

She lifted her head to look at him. "How can I get past them when they never stop coming? As long as the sun continues to set, I will continue to be broken." Velena choked on her own words. "I'm broken. There's something wrong with me. I know it's wrong to dwell on these things, but I don't know how…I don't know how to be you. I'm not ready to die, Tristan, I'm just not!" hot tears stained her dress, burying her face in her hands, she wept.

Tristan's throat was in a vice. *Oh God, I'm so inadequate! Save her! Save her not because she's good, but because You are! Show her your goodness and mercy. Please. Please. Please!*

Tristan's thoughts remained his own until he finally received the words, and the voice with which to speak them. Peace came and his confidence grew—not in himself, but in what he was certain God was going to do through him. Tristan reached out his hands and laid them awkwardly upon her raised knees, praying silently as though his very life depended on it.

"Velena, you've been afraid of death for so long. Velena, look at me," he said pulling her hands from her face. "Haven't you any idea that you're dead already? Dead in your trespasses and sins. If you died tonight, your soul would be lost and separated from God for all eternity. Why should you fear the Plague? God doesn't hate…"

"He does! Yes, He does. How can you say He doesn't hate us when He's punishing us like this?"

"Does your father hate the people who work for him?"

"What?"

"When he holds court, and someone is brought before him

who is deserving of punishment, is he wrong to execute that punishment? Does he hate the man he's punishing?"

"No."

"That man would be getting what he deserves because of his own actions. It doesn't make your father hateful or cruel to execute justice. Neither does it make God cruel to do the same. He's still a merciful God, compassionate and good. The Scriptures say in Ezekiel, *Do I have any pleasure in the death of the wicked, declares the Lord God, rather than that he should turn from his ways and live?* He takes no pleasure in the death of the wicked, but for those who die that know Him, it is pleasures for ever more. In Him is rest, Velena—perfect rest. The kind of rest you've been looking for—the kind you've needed all this while."

"If only," she said wistfully. "But it's too late for me now. I've denied Him. I'm an apostate."

"You're no such thing. You've only been ignorant of the truth—and afraid. First John says, *love has been perfected among us in this: that we may have boldness in the day of judgment; because as He is, so are we in this world. There is no fear in love; but perfect love casts out fear, because fear involves torment. But he who fears has not been made perfect in love. We love Him because He first loved us.* So you see, it's not too late, because you loving God is not dependent on you—but on Him. If He loves you, then He will make you capable of the same."

Velena listened. Tristan had her full attention, as he presented her with promise after promise from God's Holy Word—Scriptures that she'd never heard spoken before, about repentance, mercy, and rest. At first, her spirit fought against his words and wrestled against the truth of what he was saying, until all at once she knew she'd been defeated. Waves of peace began to flood over her soul, caressing her battered mind, and attending to her wounded spirit. Conquered, she soaked in every word, until finally he stopped. Eyes upon hers, and trusting God, Tristan waited.

Velena spoke softly, "I need to confess my sins to God."

Victory! He calmly stood and left her to herself, but his heart sang and all Heaven with him. He looked on as she walked beyond his line of vision, allowing her the privacy she needed. He needed it himself, as tears of gratitude and praise spilled forth from his eyes.

"I want to show you something," he said once she'd returned.

Velena was quiet, afraid that if she moved or spoke, the peace of the moment might pass.

"It's in my room," he said, wondering if she was feeling self-conscious.

"What is it?"

"Better to show you." It would have been inappropriate for Tristan to hold her hand, so he guided her by the elbow, else she would stay rooted to the ground.

As she allowed herself to be led back to the horse, she felt as if her eyes were not as they had been, as if she was seeing the world for the first time, propelled by the outstretched arm of the One who was introducing her to something she had never known before—joy.

proclaim it

"Tristan! Oh my word, how did you get this? Do you know what could happen if the wrong person were to find out?"

Tristan nodded solemnly as he took the leather bound book from Velena's hands, "I know what would happen."

"So this is what the friar gave you."

"He slipped it into my satchel as I was leaving."

Velena stood across from him, unsure of her next move. She didn't want Daisy to catch her in his room alone, but she wanted so much to sit and pepper Tristan with a hundred questions; how could she leave now?

"A Bible all your own. Does this make us heretics?"

"The truth of it definitely makes some people heretics, but only those who preach something other than these words."

"Is this how you knew to quote King David and all the rest?"

"Yes." Tristan smiled, wanting to grab Velena and swing her around the room for the joy of the moment, but he still felt that he might need to tread lightly, afraid he might scare her away with too much enthusiasm. But his fears were for nothing, for Velena was near bursting inside with anticipation.

"Wisdom. True wisdom right here—right in front of me! Nobody gets to see this, and you've had it all this time." There was nothing accusing in her tone. "How can such things ensure us a place in Heaven? I want to know!"

"I'll tell you."

A cloud passed over her face. "The priests should have told me—told us all. A curse on them for keeping God's Word under lock and key. They keep all the saints to themselves and the blessed Virgin from our embrace."

"No, Velena. It's not the saints or the Virgin that they withhold. They use the saints and Mary to distract us from the simplicity of God's Word. They've put them front and center and made them barriers to our understanding. And worse, they promise to deliver us from our sins by tossing us ropes made of writs of salvation. As if our money could buy us a place in Heaven. It's only Jesus that we need! Please hear me." *Please, Lord, let her hear me.*

Tristan continued, "In plain sight they've held Him up on a cross for us all to see. It's been Him all along! I can show Him to you."

Tristan could no longer contain the excitement in his voice. "He's not on the cross, He's here...here on these pages."

Velena walked over to the door and peeked her head out into the hall. Satisfied, she closed herself in and sat down cross-legged with her back to the wall. "Tell me something else. Anything."

Tristan joined her on the floor. "Mary didn't stay a virgin."

"What?!" Velena laughed

"Joseph only kept away from her until after Jesus was born. Jesus had half brothers and sisters."

"How many?"

"It doesn't say, but two of them wrote books in the Bible."

"No."

"Yes."

"What else?"

"We don't need priests for confession."

"So you've said, but why?"

"Because Jesus is our high priest. In first Timothy it says, *for there is one God and one mediator between God and men, the man Christ Jesus.* And in Hebrews it says, *therefore, since we have a great high priest who has passed through the heavens, Jesus the Son of God, let us hold fast our confession. For we do not have a high priest who cannot sympathize with our weaknesses, but*

One who has been tempted in all things as we are, yet without sin. Therefore, let us draw near with confidence to the throne of grace, so that we may receive mercy and find grace to help in time of need."

"That's beautiful."

"I used to read this to myself every day when I first came to be here."

"I can see why. Tell me something else."

"We can't earn our way into Heaven as the Church would have us believe—holding our sins over us as leverage for obedience, not to God but to themselves. We are all born into sin. Our hearts are continually evil and we can never be good enough. No amount of penance will buy us in."

"Then how can we be saved?"

"A better question you've never asked! *If you believe in your heart and confess with your mouth that Jesus is Lord you'll be saved.* Romans."

"That's all?"

"Have you repented?"

"Yes."

"Then that's all. God loves you, Velena. Almighty God loves you—the Father, Himself! And He *is* good."

"I want to believe that," Velena said, once again feeling very vulnerable and unworthy to be coming before Him now. She wanted so much to know that He was good, and He'd have to be if there was any hope of her being accepted, as wretched and broken as she was. Did He really love her, even after she'd denied Him? "Could you show me where...where it...I mean, does it actually say so somewhere?"

"Here look what it says in John. I can translate it for you, if you'd like."

"It's all right. I'd like to try it, myself."

"Tristan smiled his approval."

"If you abide in Me, and My words abide in you, ask whatever you wish, and it will be done for you. My Father is glorified by this, that you bear much fruit, and so prove to be My disciples. Just as the Father has loved Me, I have also loved you; abide in my love. If you keep My commandments, you will abide in My love;

131

just as I have kept My Father's commandments and abide in His love. These things I have spoken to you so that My joy may be in you, and that your joy may be made full."

"What are you thinking?" Tristan asked after she failed to say anything for several moments.

"I don't know."

"Impossible."

Velena laughed. "I don't know. I suppose…I suppose I'm just wondering how to do it. For the first time in a long time, I don't feel afraid. The test of that will be tonight, and I don't know about tomorrow, but right now…I'm not afraid to die, Tristan." Velena's face was aglow with new joy. "If this is all true then…"

"It is."

"Then, okay."

"Okay, what?"

"I believe it."

"You do?"

"I do!" Velena laughed and covered her face with her hands trying to suppress the enormity of her smile, and when that wasn't enough she brought her knees up and buried her face in her skirts.

Finally, she peeked out. "Say something."

Tristan jumped up with a startling shout. "Huzzah! "Then confess it Velena! Right out the window!"

Velena stood then, intent on racing to the far side of his room, but was caught up by the wrist.

"Better not do it out my window." They both turned and ran for the hall and the window at the far end opposite the staircase.

Velena was no longer behind prison bars; she was free, "I believe!!" she shouted into the wind. "I believe," she whispered to herself, feeling tears of joy slipping down her cheeks.

She waved at Jonas and Kat below, who giggled in return. She turned around to face Tristan, resting her hands on the edge of the windowsill behind her. He had tears in his eyes.

"What do you want to do now?"

"Will you read me some more?"

"Get comfortable."

in confidence

Daisy let down Velena's hair and began running her brush through it in long drawn out strokes until it hung smooth and glossy. Dividing it into three pieces, she began plaiting the length of it until she had one long, thick plait. All the while Velena was trying to decide how she was going to meet with Tristan in his solar again without arousing the wrong kind of suspicions.

"There you go," Daisy said, finally finishing. She came around to unbutton Velena's cuffs, but felt her pull away. If she undressed now, that would definitely pose a problem to her being able to dress herself again later without waking Daisy, and even if she forwent her day clothes for her robe, if they were discovered, she'd not be able to explain it away.

"No thank you, Daisy. I'll not be undressing quite yet."

"It'll be dark soon," Daisy replied, confused.

Velena made a decision and hoped it would not prove to be unwise. "There's something I need to tell you—and not tell you. In both cases, and either way, I need your absolute silence about the matter you know, and the matter you won't—or don't, rather. Because it's best you don't know, which is why I won't tell you."

"I don't understand."

"I'm going to Tristan's solar tonight..."

"You'll do no such thing!"

Velena pushed on; she had no choice now, "And not just for tonight, but often, I should think."

"Have you gone mad?"

"It's not for any reasons you're thinking, Daisy, of course. Of course not, rather. I'm making a mess of things, so please just hear me out before you say anything else."

Daisy left Velena at the desk chair and sat down upon the bed, arms crossed. "All right."

"Thank you. I know that you worry about my friendship with Tristan, so let me confirm to you once again, that we are not in love with one another. I am betrothed to Peter, and will remain faithfully his and no others. Tristan is none to me but a dear, dear brother."

Daisy raised an eyebrow.

"In any case there is a…a book. It's a special book that Tristan brought back with him after his mother died, and I would like to read it—with him, that is."

"A book. Pardon me for speaking my mind, but couldn't he just lend it to you? Must he lure you into his solar to do so?"

Velena swallowed a few choice words, knowing she needed Daisy's loyalty. "Yes, I know he would, but the problem is that I don't really understand it, myself, and I would like his commentary on the subject.

"Is it in another language?"

"Yes," she answered truthfully.

Daisy uncrossed her arms, but still appeared ill at ease. "Is the hall so unfit for your book study, my Lady, because if you were caught…"

"I won't be."

"But if ever you were, and your father knew I'd let you, he'd have me lashed for sure."

"I would never let them happen. You know how much you mean to me. The reason we can't sit out in the open has to do with that part that it's best you don't know about. No one ever comes up to my solar, but just in case, all I'd want you to do is say that I have a headache and don't wish to be disturbed. I'll limit myself to one hour. Enough time to read, but not enough time to grow idle into…other things. Which, of course, we never would."

"He's a man."

"He's Tristan, and if you're honest with yourself, you know you trust him just the same as I."

Daisy looked down uncertainly, choosing to play with the ends of her blond hair instead of responding.

"Will you keep my secret? I won't force you. This matter is very delicate and important to me. Is what I've asked suitable to you?"

None of it's suitable, my lady, but I'll do as you wish. I know your intentions are innocent—even if the situation is not, pardon my candor."

Velena fought the urge to roll her eyes, as Daisy was nothing, if not candid. "Thank you. I've been stewing about how to tell you all evening. But, now you know and I feel much better about the whole thing." Velena walked over to squeeze both her hands, and then turned to leave the room.

"Yes, my lady, but promise me," she called out before Velena could reach the door, "Promise me that it's not a book of witch craft or any other such devilry. I do think highly of Lord Tristan, but I'd hate to think that I'd sat idly by while he deceived us all and introduced you into dark things. For it to be illegal it must be very bad indeed." Daisy stood then, wringing her hands and tears in her eyes.

"No, Daisy." Velena ran back, hugging her tightly. "You're too clever for me to keep secrets from. It is illegal for us to have it, but there's no darkness in it. I promise you that! I feel as though I've finally met God. All this time I didn't know Him. Have you met God Daisy?"

"I'm a God fearing woman if that's what you mean?"

"I...I don't know if that's what I mean. But you don't need to worry about me."

Daisy kissed her mistress's cheek and walked over to a shelf where she had a basket of sewing and some candles. "I'll sit up and wait for you—but only for one hour," Daisy said, pointed a finger at Velena's chest, "one hour."

Velena smiled. "I'll leave it to you to keep track of the time;

come and get me when the hour's up. That way you know I won't take advantage of you. Don't knock, just open the door."

Daisy nodded as Velena disappeared into the hallway. Reaching for a candle, she took the knife hanging from her belt and cut down the wick so that it would go out in approximately an hours" time. She wasn't happy with the situation, but something in her mistress' face had convinced her. Daisy wasn't sure if Velena had taken off a mask or put a face on, but whatever it was, far be it for Daisy to be left out of a good intrigue.

As the hour dragged on for Daisy, it couldn't have passed more quickly for Velena and Tristan. Tristan decided to start their new journey in the book of Hebrews, lingering on passages that had brought him the most encouragement during his initial time of grief, showing her how to apply the spiritual salve to her wounds through the truths of God's Word.

Tristan's pain was not gone, but he held a perspective of it that Velena had not been able to achieve—before now. For finally, here in this candle lit room, Velena's faith burned brighter then she'd ever thought possible.

Meanwhile, Daisy's short wicked candle had gone out, so now outside Tristan's door, she stood with one hand laid upon the handle and the other across her eyes. Inhaling, she thrust the door open wide, thoroughly surprising those on the other side.

She spoke in a rushed sort of whisper. "Excuse me, my lady, but the hour is up."

"Daisy, you silly thing, take your hand away from your eyes. We're quite decent."

Daisy lowered her hand, thankful that the dim lighting hid the blush that had risen to her cheeks. "Of course you are," she stammered.

"Indeed." Velena tried without success to keep a straight face, and almost lost it all together when she looked over to see Tristan's eyes watering from trying to stifle his laughter from becoming anything louder than a whispers' worth in volume.

"Lady Velena, please hurry. Need I remind you that the door is still wide open and you could be discovered at any moment. I'll not allow you more time; this hour, alone, has felt like days."

Velena arose from her place at the desk, and smiled her goodbyes to Tristan who'd been listening to her read from his place on the bed.

Tristan got up to see them to the door, wearing a grin especially meant for Daisy. "You don't need to worry about your mistress; she's safe with me."

"She'd better be…because I know people," she said with scowl.

"You know people, huh. Are you threatening me?" Tristan almost laughed outright but had the sense to hold back."

"Whatever it takes."

Velena was already half way down the hall before she noticed that Daisy hadn't followed. "Come away from there, Daisy," she hissed.

But Tristan only held up his hand for her to be patient. "Your threat goes a long way in letting me know how much you love her. We have that in common, so I promise you…she's safe with me."

Tristan could tell she wasn't sure what to say next, so he bid her a quick goodnight and shut the door without waiting for a response.

Daisy stared blankly at the wooden barrier before padding after Velena.

"What did he say to you," Velena whispered from her doorway.

"That he loves you madly!"

Velena smirked.

"That you're safe with him."

"I told you I was," Velena whispered, stepping aside to allow Daisy entrance. Quickly, she rushed through the motions of getting ready for bed, anxious for the first time in two years to get to sleep. She climbed under her covers wondering if all the excitement of the day would still end up keeping her awake, but it wouldn't be so. No sooner had her head hit her pillow, did she fall into a dreamless sea of rest, hidden in her Savior's tabernacle—where she could finally lay her burdens down.

pleasant days

Holding a corner in each hand, Daisy helped Velena lay out a gray and white striped blanket just up from the creek. This place had quickly become Tristan and Velena's favorite spot.

Tristan claimed a space for himself, laying back upon his arms and closing his eyes as if ready for a nap.

"I hate to see this sort of weather end," Velena said staring down at the water, "I've never been much for the cold. What I wouldn't give for a good foot soak."

"That sounds lovely," Daisy agreed, sitting beside Tristan.

"And bear your ankles? Really girls, you're too scandalous for my taste."

Daisy giggled.

Velena complained. "Why is it that a man can walk around half naked and a woman can't even show her ankles—or her arms for that matter? Do you know how hot these tunics can be?"

"When have I ever walked around half naked?" Tristan answered, not bothering to open his eyes.

"Never, I hope," Daisy quipped.

Velena only smiled. "Would a woman's ankles really drive a man to distraction?"

Tristan pulled out a handkerchief from somewhere inside his tunic and flung it over his eyes to block out the light, "Depends on which woman and which ankles."

"As if they're detached."

"No, but if the ankle is lovely but the woman is homely, I may have to find a beautiful woman to look at so that I could simultaneously admire the ankle—if it were to be a proper distraction."

"That's ridiculous. If you then found yourself impassioned, who would you choose to be with...the beautiful woman or the owner of the ankle, for it would be partly the ankle that gained your interest."

"How are the ankles of the beautiful woman?"

"By your very scenario they are hideous or you wouldn't have suggested two separate women."

"Quite right." Tristan took a moment to clear his throat. "Probably the beautiful woman."

"Why?" Daisy asked, feeling the sudden urge to check the size of her own ankles.

"Well, you see," Tristan said, raising a corner of his hankie so he could peek out at her, "it's not a woman's ankles that *interests* me."

Daisy laughed, pushing the handkerchief back down over his face as if to smother him, triggering a brief tug of war that ended with Tristan shoving the offending piece of material back inside his tunic for safe keeping.

"What is it that...*interests* you?" Velena interrupted, unable to put aside her curiosity.

Tristan's face turned several shades of red just before dropping his eyes below her neckline for the briefest of moments. "Never mind about that," he said laying back again.

Daisy gasped. "Watch yourself!"

"Me? I didn't bring any of this up in the first place. Awkward conversations are the product of women prattling on about things they shouldn't."

"Men talk about things they shouldn't," Velena defended, still deciding whether or not to comment on his choice of the word *prattling*.

"Yes, but it's never awkward." Tristan looked to Daisy and shook his head back and forth, "There's just something about your mistress that necessitates I tell her everything I'm thinking."

"Surely not everything," Daisy interrupted.

"Well, a fair amount, and that's still an understatement."

"By the very nature of your relationship being what it is and what it shouldn't be, you really ought to learn to keep some things to yourself. It's called self-control," Daisy said pertly.

Tristan raised to one elbow. "So, I shouldn't tell you how attracted I am to women with blond hair and dimples, then," he said leaning forward to tug at her hair.

Daisy slapped at his hand and pulled away. "I don't know about you, my lady" she said rising to her feet, "but my quota for Tristan time has been filled; kindly hand me that basket, good sir."

"Where are you going?" Velena asked in surprise.

"To look for mushrooms—the poisonous kind."

Velena laughed, watching her traipse off further into the woods. "I don't know why you tease her like that; she only barely likes you."

"Barely liking me is better than hardly liking me."

"I think it's the other way around," Velena teased.

"I think it was you that scared her away with your inappropriate questions."

"You don't have to answer them."

Tristan chuckled, "Do you know it never crosses my mind to talk with anyone else about a tenth of what I share with you. I mean, how in the world do you get me to talk about what feature I like in a woman?"

"You mean which *features*—there are two."

Tristan blushed again, but to his credit, managed to maintain eye contact, "Yes there are. But this is exactly what I mean," he said, laying back upon the blanket.

Velena smiled, then looked down to study her own petite figure.

Tristan looked away, pretending not to notice.

"I suppose this means I won't please a man."

"Well, I wasn't going to say anything."

Velena kicked at his foot. "You're horrible!"

He smiled, "I'm sure your intended will be very happy with you. In the meantime, though, I think we've determined that your ankles are not a threat to my self-control."

"Still don't look," she warned with a laugh, sitting down with her back turned toward him. She removed her shoes and stockings out from beneath her tunic and sighed with pleasure, relishing the feel of the cool water rushing over her bare feet.

Tristan just smiled and settled back again, re-positioning his handkerchief over his eyes and wondering what unlikely conversations would come up next.

doubts

Velena flounced into her father's solar, happy to escape the cold, rainy weather from outside. It was particularly quiet as most had already gone on ahead to the great hall for the evening meal. There was only the wardrober and several valets present, and even they were on their way out. Velena looked disappointed and almost turned to leave when she heard Tristan clearing his throat.

She turned about but didn't see him. "Tristan is that you?"

"Out in a moment," he called, his voice echoing from inside the garderobe.[11] After a short moment he walked out, adjusting his stockings with one hand and holding her father's accounting book with the other.

"Do you normally do your work while doing your *business?*"

"No point in wasting time."

Velena scrunched up her nose in disgust, but quickly changed the subject as soon as she remembered why she'd been looking for him.

"What do you think?" she said proudly, producing a piece of paper she'd hidden inside her cloak.

Tristan was still looking over some numbers as he walked by and sat down. "I think, that despite any losses that your father may have accrued over these last two years, he still makes an extraordinary amount of money, and that your intended can count his blessings that he's marrying into it."

Velena rolled her eyes. "I meant for you to look at my drawing."

Tristan raised his head, "Hm. That's very good; I like it. Is it a snake of some sort?"

"It's the creek."

"That was my second guess."

"Very funny. It's your birthday gift. Congratulations on staying alive until you were eighteen," she teased.

"I never thought I'd hear you joke about death."

"I'm not; I'm celebrating your life—though I have a mind to give my drawing to someone else who'll appreciate it. Daisy might."

"Don't do that," he said snatching it from her hands with a smile. "I knew what it was. Thank you."

"You're welcome. Now put your numbers aside; everyone's left already. Walk me to the hall?"

Tristan looked around as if noticing for the first time. "Is it Vespers already?"

He tucked Velena's picture in between the pages of her father's ledger and placed it back on the shelf before grabbing his cloak and following her out into the rain.

"Why do you always call him my *intended?*" Velena asked.

"That's what he is?"

"I just think it's funny that you always refer to him as that and not by his name."

"Like you do with *Isulte.*"

Velena giggled. "I suppose I do that, don't I?"

Tristan looked over in amusement. "You do realize that most everything you accuse me of, you're guilty of yourself."

"You expect my double standards to change?"

"After two years, I should know better."

"So why do we do that then—not say their names? I was wondering, because whenever you refer to Peter as my intended it almost sounds as if you're belittling him. Do I do that with Isulte?"

"No, not that I've noticed."

"Good. I know you still hope to see her again."

"I never really had hope of that, but thank you for hoping for me."

Velena looked sympathetic as they walked the remaining distance in silence. The bailey was empty and they could hear the hall alive with reveling. In unison, the men were pounding the tables with the butts of their knives, shouting for their dinner and laughing at each other's clever poetry attempts to coax the meal out from the kitchen faster.

Velena smiled at the familiar sounds of men at play. She started up the steps, but Tristan held back. "What's the matter?"

"The truth is, Velena, Isulte is far away and probably married by now. You're the one I stand to lose someday."

"You're not going to lose me!" Velena protested as Tristan joined her on the top step, their two bodies framed in the open doorway.

"Every day spent with you is a day that moves us closer to Peter's return. There, I said it. Peter. I don't like saying his name because he's the wedge that will separate us. And all this, that we have here, will be a thing of the past, and it…well, it depresses me," he said, wrinkling up his nose as if the thought stank just to say it.

"Peter's coming won't change anything," Velena protested.

"You've really never given this a second thought?"

"What's to think about? There's no act of wrong in our friendship."

"I know that, but your father and my Uncle Rolland trust us, and they give us little notice as they're busy with their own affairs, and wouldn't think to suspect us of anything else. But when your uncle comes with Peter, their affairs will revolve around you, and they're sure to notice a great many things. This isn't normal, Velena, surely you know that—a man and a woman being friends as we are."

"You're like my brother."

"But I'm not your brother, and Peter won't be sympathetic to your version of family."

"He can't order me not to have friends."

"Yes, he can."

"Well—he won't."

"If you were my wife and you had a *friend* as we are friends, I would most definitely put an end to it. I blame myself for getting too close."

Velena cocked her head to one side in frustration. "We won't be able to meet in your room anymore, but I don't see why we can't enjoy each other's company as we've always done."

"Do you think we'll be living in the same house when you marry? And married woman don't usually receive social calls from men."

Velena's thoughts began to go in different directions as she began to think about the reality of what Tristan was trying to say. Yet, here he stood in front of her, faithful and familiar, and she really couldn't picture life without him.

"Do you hate Peter then?"

"No, only the general idea of you marrying someone."

Velena put her hands on her hips and leaned forward, playfully suspicious. "Someone or someone else."

Then laughing at his expression, she walked out of the rain and into the hall, immediately taken up into the commotion.

Not to be left behind, he quickly caught up, speaking almost directly into her ear so she could hear him, for the merrymaking was still in full swing, as the men continued belting out song after song.

"That is not at all what I meant."

"What is that supposed to mean?" Velena quipped, "Why wouldn't you want to marry me? Daisy's always telling me that you do," she said, raising her hand to acknowledge her lady's maid who was now waving to her from one of the lower tables at the head of the room.

"Would you want to marry me?" he threw back.

Velena laughed before she could think better of it, and then shook her head. "Never mind. A sister cannot marry her brother; it would be—annoying."

"Among other things," Tristan mumbled.

"Let's not talk about my *intended* right now, for that's all he is. I defy all of your very logical arguments and choose to believe you're wrong—very, very wrong. You'll see." Velena gave him a reassuring look and then left him there, staring after her.

Tristan never regretted the attachment he'd formed with Velena, but there was a part of him that wondered if he was holding on too tightly. He knew her absence would create a void in his life that he didn't care to dwell on. He didn't think he was in love with her, but was that only because he compared his feelings to that of what he'd felt for Isulte.

He smiled at Velena's name for her, but then knit his brow in confusion. How could he compare what he'd felt for Gwenhavare with what he felt for Velena? He knew next to nothing about her, the entire basis for his feelings resting on one party along with a few brief hellos—and yet he called that love.

He knew every aspect of the woman now taking her seat at the dais. He loved her too, but it was different. Which emotion was true? Was what he felt for Gwenhavare really infatuation? Was this woman, this sister in the Lord, this friend—was this love the real thing, only he didn't recognize it? He told Velena once that love was a choice. Did he have a choice?

Suddenly, he looked around the hall, embarrassed by his thoughts, realizing how it must look to everyone else to have him standing there staring after her. Quickly, he moved forward to sit beside her, stewing over his thoughts, now wishing he were close enough to someone else to share them with.

Someone else…someone else! Of course, what was he thinking? Velena was engaged to someone else. What choice did he have to wrestle with? None. There was no choice to be made; she was betrothed to another! He laughed at himself. He needn't overly examine his feelings, for it would be of no benefit to fancy himself in love with her now, or worse, when she was actually married and those thoughts could mature into something sinful.

He had no desire to covet another man's wife. He only wanted Velena to be happy. He wanted God's choice for her, and if God was sovereign, and he knew He was, then this meant Peter. He was her betrothed. Tristan determined to start praying for him during his runs. He didn't know how much of Velena he would lose to this marriage, but he knew going down the rabbit trail he'd just been on, was a sure way to losing everything.

news

A now seven-year-old Jonas sat atop Bowan's shoulders thumping his thighs with boy sized fists as feathers flew wildly about them. It was a good old-fashioned cockfight, and those standing by were calling out in approval as bets were placed on their favorite bird. Even ten-year-old Navarre was allowed to place a small bet.

Kat's blond hair hung across her face as she ran around the gated circle egging on the fight. "Come on Blackie! Come on; you can do it!" she called out.

"Don't listen to her Agricola," Jonas screamed, "claw his eyes out!"

Bowan laughed out loud at his little friend, enjoying every moment.

As if in answer to the boy's call the brown cock made a quick pivot and jumped onto the back of Blackie who was too late to avert the move. Agricola's claws sunk in deep, tearing at the flesh beneath his nails before being tossed from his opponent's back.

Velena cupped her hands in front of her mouth, cheering on Kat's Blackie as Daisy tried to smother her mouth with a hand. She was calling out the name of Bowan's favorite instead, and both girls were having great fun laughing and enjoying the company around them. This was especially true of a dimple-cheeked Daisy who exchanged smiles and glances with Bowan at every spare moment.

Now recovered, Blackie turned to face the mighty Agricola, both cocks rushing in at once, only to meet in the air to the delighted applause of all. Just then, her father's valet, Geoffrey, approached Velena from behind.

"Pardon, my lady, but your father wishes an audience with you."

What horrible timing. Velena opened her mouth in protest, looking from him to the exciting scene still playing out in the circle, but knew better than to do anything other than acquiesce. "Of course, where is he?"

"In his solar, my lady."

"Kat, tell me if Blackie wins," she shouted back over her shoulder.

"You mean *when* he wins. Come on Blackie!"

Velena smiled, turning to leave, when she noticed Geoffrey lingering behind. Nothing like a good cockfight to divert one's attention.

She wasn't two steps from the door of the keep when Tristan emerged first, followed by a man Velena had never seen before. Tristan gave her a wink, as if to say all was well, as he brushed passed her towards the hall—stranger in tow.

The last time Velena had seen a stranger her heart had been beating so fast she thought it might fly from her chest. This time Velena only smiled to herself, grateful that the flutter she felt was born of excitement and not fear. Almighty God was her resting place now.

"You called for me, Father," she said, rushing in. "Who was the man I saw walking out with Tristan?"

"He's brought word from Magnus. Your uncle has survived the Plague and is on his way here."

Velena inhaled sharply. "Here? Praise God!"

"Yes, I figured if anyone could live through death it would be him—him and the other cockroaches."

"Father!"

Sir Richard let out a low chuckle, then motioned for her to be seated, "I consented to your marrying Peter because of your mother, not because of her intolerable brother."

"Peter's alive? You know this for sure?"

"The letter didn't say, truth be told, but I don't know why else Magnus would be coming if he wasn't. My guess is that your cousin Peter is coming for his bride." The Baron stroked his beard and sighed.

"You say it as though you disapprove."

"No." Sir Richard brushed her comment aside. "Well, maybe a little. You're eighteen now; I don't want an old maid on my hands," he teased, "but I'll be missing you when you gone."

Gone?

"But don't listen to me, it's you I want to be happy. What say you?"

"I'm not sure what to say; it seems a lifetime since I've seen him."

"That's the truth. We'll hold back on the wedding for a week, or even a fortnight if you'd like, so you have time to get used to each other, if that will make you more comfortable. We're in no hurry."

"Thank you," Velena said, fingering a splinter of wood coming up from the table.

"Is there something else on your mind?" her father asked.

"I was wondering if it was safe to go back with him. Does the letter say anything about the Plague? Is it over?"

"I suspect we'll hear more about that when they arrive. I'd like to have him stay here awhile, but we'll cross that bridge when we come to it. Let's first think of settling them all in. This is no Landerhill, so we're short on space. We're at half capacity in the barracks, so it shouldn't be too much of a problem, but just in case, let's prepare the stables for any overflow of squires. Have some men clean out a few stalls and lay some bedding down—as warm as they can make it; the nights are still plenty cold. Tristan will join us here in my solar, so that his room can be made ready for your aunt and uncle. Peter...and Stuart will stay in there as well, I suspect. Let Tristan know for me."

"Stuart." Velena smiled as she said his name. "I won't know what to do with myself. When will they arrive?"

"Tomorrow—late. We'll have a late dinner to accommodate them."

"So soon!"

"The man he sent was only a day ahead of him. And it's a good thing too; you're no good at waiting."

Velena scrambled out from behind the bench and flung her arms around her father's neck. He was right after all, for even now, the anticipation was torture. Velena left relieved that there was so much to keep her busy or else she'd have to cement herself to the ramparts as a look out.

"May I go?"

"By all means, go…go, before I'm smothered to death." Sir Richard chuckled.

Velena bounded from the keep at a full run, only to encounter a very enthusiastic Kat. The fight was over and black and brown feathers littered the ground everywhere. The crowd was now dissipating as they laughed and paid out or collected what money they'd wagered on the winning bird.

"He won, Lady Velena, he won! Blackie beat the feathers off of old Agricola."

"I never had a better bird," Jonas bemoaned to Navarre who, having long accepted the younger boy's hero worship for holding his dream job, patted his friend on the shoulder, while fingering two small farthings in his other hand. Jonas noticed. "You bet against Agricola? Do you like my sister, or something?"

Navarre shrugged his shoulders and Katrina blushed. "Don't be mad, Jonas. You can half one of my farthings."

Velena held back a laugh. "Sorry you lost, Jonas. I'm on my way to the stables; you're welcome to accompany me if you'd like."

"No thanks. I'm going to take him on over to the kitchen. At least he'll make a good meal."

Velena chuckled. "I'm sure he will."

anticipation

Had the village the benefit of a church, it's bells would have rung out Vespers. The sun was now low in the sky, and the evening air was chilly, but only Velena's exposed face suffered the effects of it as she adjusted her fur-lined cloak to fit snugly about her shoulders.

Velena had told herself to keep busy, but preparations for Peter's arrival had all been made in record time. At first she'd taken to pacing the floor in her solar, wondering what it would be like to see him again.

After noticing the definitive trail that she was leaving among the rushes that lay strewn upon the stone floor, she'd wandered about aimlessly until she found herself on the ramparts. She looked out past the forest trees, willing the traveling party to both come in great haste, and to delay, so that she'd have time to get a handle of her nerves. She rested her elbows upon the embrasure,[12] leaning her head against the side of the stone protrusion.

After a bit, her thoughts drifted toward Tristan and what this would mean for them. Just then, she heard a familiar whistle as he strolled along the curtain wall in her direction. *Speak of the devil.*

"So, we're to have guests," he stated without emotion, as though the information held no meaning for him.

"Seems hard to believe they're finally coming."

"Did your father say who among your uncle's family is making the journey?"

"I would assume, all of them—Peter, Stuart, and their mother."

"Tristan raised his eyebrows, "They all survived? That's amazing."

"Well, I don't actually know for certain, but he didn't write otherwise."

"Velena."

"What?"

"Your uncle may not have wanted to write of his losses in a letter."

"I think he would have said something."

"Maybe—it's just not that likely for an entire family to survive. I just want you to be prepared."

Velena turned her gaze back out toward the trees, making no motion to continue with the conversation.

"Are you all right?" he finally asked.

"Are you?"

"I asked first."

"Yes. I was just thinking about my mother. You're right, of course. I need to prepare myself. The Plague has taken from us all."

Tristan regretted his words, "Who knows? Perhaps I'm wrong. You could be very happily surprised. You must be looking forward to seeing your intended—Peter, I mean." Tristan smiled, catching himself.

"I don't know what to feel. To be honest, I haven't thought about him in a long time. I was never as close to Peter as I was to Stuart. We were closer in age and we used to play together as children. Peter is eight years my senior and was already a page in someone else's household by the time I was born. And on his visits home, he always had better things to do then to play hide and seek with his silly female cousin. It wasn't until I turned thirteen that he paid the least bit of attention to me."

Tristan crossed his arms under his cloak. "That's completely understandable. There's hardly a girl that exists that's worth paying attention to until she's thirteen."

Velena laughed despite herself. "Even then, I think it was because our fathers had made the arrangement. He was always kind to me, but I could never tell if he was really pleased with our betrothal or not. Velena paused. "Sorry. I've told you all this before."

"Yes…you have, so what's really bothering you?" Tristan leaned his head against the merlon,[13] turning sideways so he could give her his full attention.

"He's had to wait so long."

"You're eighteen, not eighty."

"Still, I half expect him to arrive married to someone else."

"I doubt he'd come if that were true."

Velena's eyes appeared glassy, but she didn't cry.

"Velena, you're worth having, and worth waiting for. Don't let anyone tell you any different."

"It means a lot for you to say so. I know how you feel about his coming. Thank you for understanding." Velena took a deep breath before turning her back on the world beyond the wall, falling into an easy step beside her friend. "When you came to visit Landerhill all those years ago with your Uncle Rolland, did you get along with Peter and Stuart? I don't remember too much about our interacting with you."

"That would be because you didn't—other than at the cockfight—which I won."

"I do remember that," Velena interrupted.

"Well, it was a fight to remember. The one the children had going on here today was particularly reminiscent of that time. But, no, other than that brief interlude with you all, I spent most of my time with Squire Rowan, who was only a page at the time."

"Rowan!" The corners of her mouth turned up as a bright smile lit her face, followed by a crinkling up of her nose "What a tease. I can't tell you how much I enjoyed him despite it though. I have so many memories with him and Stuart, and Jaren. I know you know about Rowan, but Jaren was also a squire at my uncle's manor.

"I remember him."

"His brother is here you know."

"I didn't. Who is he?"

"Sir Andret."

"Really?"

"Yes, and there's also a third older brother, Sir Makaias. He's already a knight."

"The *Sir* before his name tipped me off."

Velena pushed him in the shoulder, and then grew serious. "He's with Brit in Calais. I think if they were still alive, we would have heard something of them by now."

"You can still hope."

"I do," she said looking over at him, "I do."

In silence, they walked back to the keep. Velena's thoughts were so full of tomorrow that she forgot to turn the conversation back to Tristan, and how he was feeling about her uncle coming. She knew it would bring changes, but she refused to think they'd be as drastic as Tristan might think.

From his end, Tristan juggled the idea of inviting Velena back to his solar for one last time in the Word, but he knew he needed some moments to himself. When Peter arrived, he'd have to diminish. He knew it was the right and natural thing to do, but it grieved him all the same.

---

[12] **Embrasure:** The opening between the two upright solid portions (merlons) of a battlement.

[13] **Merlon:** The solid upright portion of a battlement.

reoccurring dreams

Tristan had been up half the night tossing and turning, trying to convince himself that, come morning, everything would be fine and as it should be. He'd been just about ready to pull his hair out, when he remembered where he ought to be.

On his knees beside the bed, Tristan bore his soul to God—his concerns, his fears, his anxieties—he lay them all upon the altar. He realized that although his initial intention of bringing Velena into a closer relationship with Jesus was admirable, he'd allowed himself to grow less dependent on His Savior, in favor of leaning more and more on Velena for his emotional well-being.

He was ashamed of it and repented then and there, placing her too upon the altar, trusting that only there would she truly remain blessed. Finally, he crawled back into bed and slept.

He'd dreamed that he and Velena were back upon the ramparts—the sky was clear, the night crisp. Not even a breeze dared flutter Velena's loose strands of hair. She stood before him wearing an expression that he could only describe as troubled.

She was beautiful there in the moonlight; he felt the urge to hold her and tell her everything was going to be all right, but he was hesitant to touch her. So, he stood his ground, watching her as she spoke of things that he'd no longer remember come morning.

As the dream drew to a close, she startled him by repeating the words from the first dream he'd ever had of her: *Walk with me.'* She held out her hand as she had before, and asked him to walk with her.

He started to take it, but then suddenly the sky was a blanket of clouds. Snow began to fall and a great wind came up between them, amassing the snow in such a way that he lost sight of her hand. He could see her face, troubled before, she was now unconcerned and peaceful despite the storm. He wanted to be where she was, but her hand was lost in white.

He awoke, trying to make sense of the dream, but he drifted off again, unsatisfied. Later, he stood at his desk, carefully stacking the few papers that he'd just finished writing on. At the first light of dawn, Tristan had decided that dream or no dream, he would start this day by relying on God to provide him with the answers he needed—in His good timing.

first kisses

Velena sat at her vanity as Daisy parted her hair down the middle, and plaited one side at a time, carefully winding them up into buns just above her ears. Velena handed Daisy the golden circlet she'd been gripping, as her eyes lingered on the bed reflected in the mirror before her. She was embarrassed by her thoughts despite the fact that Daisy couldn't read them.

"What do you think of that?" Daisy said standing back inspecting her work.

"You've done a beautiful job. It's been so long since I've had my hair up; I hardly recognize myself."

"You look every bit a queen, my lady. Your hair wears the gold well; it always has. Put gold in my hair and it gets positively lost—too much yellow."

"What shall I wear? I want to wear my finest, but they might not arrive until dark, and then it'll be hardly light enough to appreciate anything I put on."

"Save your best for tomorrow morning when you'll be able to make better use of it all day. I think today you should wear something subtle in color, but perhaps more provocative in nature. The neckline of your navy tunic has always flattered you. You'll be able to see these bones here," Daisy said, gesturing to her own clavicles, "and they'll look alluring in the glow of a fireplace."

Velena couldn't help but laugh at Daisy's serious tone and far off looks, but she heartily agreed and allowed Daisy to help her dress into the simple, yet flattering gown. She hadn't been two seconds in her clothes before they heard a knock at the door.

Daisy snorted as she crossed the room to answer it, "Doesn't he know he'll not be able to do this anymore? You can get as done up as you like, but one false move while Peter's around and you'll be a spinster for sure."

"Daisy, shh."

Just as they both expected, Tristan stood on the other side of the oak barricade wearing an apologetic grin, meant especially for the moody lady in waiting. "I promise it's the last time, Daisy."

"I'll believe it when I see it—or don't see it, as I hope the case may be."

Velena came up behind her and motioned that she should carry on with her duties.

"Here." Tristan held out the papers for Velena to see, noting both her change of hairstyle, as well as choice of gown. Just one more reminder of what today would bring.

"What's this?"

"Psalms," he whispered.

Velena glanced behind her to see if Daisy had been paying attention and then turned back to Tristan with a playful smile, "All of them?"

"I have amazing abilities, and only a few of which you know about."

"Oh really." Velena looked down at the words so carefully penned in the wee hours of the morning and felt tears come to her eyes.

"Okay, well it's actually only a dismal amount, but I wanted you to have something to read and...memorize since we won't be...meeting anymore."

"Tristan." Velena wanted so much to reassure him of her loyalty and affections.

"No, truly, I'm not sulking. I only meant that we wouldn't be meeting in my solar anymore."

"You no longer have one anyway," Velena teased.

"This is true, so in the spirit of change, I think this may really work well or us. Whenever I have the chance, I'll write something out for you, and when we find some moments alone, we can discuss them. If you have questions that I can't answer, which of course will be many—that is to say the answers, not the questions, I will have my next assignment. What do you think?"

Velena couldn't believe how vulnerable he looked standing there, and it killed her to think he might no longer know his place in her life anymore. Did she know, herself?

"I think that this is very like you. It's just like you to do something like this for me." Velena's throat constricted, but she recovered with a cheeky grin. "I approve. And I also think that Daisy will be very put out that you didn't suggest this plan of action sooner. It's been a very stressful year for her."

"Amen to that," Daisy chimed in, picking up the last part of her sentence.

Tristan sidestepped Velena. "I'd like to have a word with you as well."

Daisy skulked her way over, trying to will her dimples away. She wanted to be angry with Tristan, but she had to admit that he'd kept his word, and Velena's virtue intact.

"You've faithfully kept our secret, and for that, I'm forever in your debt. You're a sweet girl, Daisy, and I want to be the first to tell you that you no longer have to sit up waiting for your mistress any longer. No more late nights, no more intrigue. What do you think of that?"

Daisy crossed herself and clasped her hands towards heaven, dimples in full bloom. "Hallelujah. I could kiss you."

Tristan raised his eyebrows as if he thought very well of himself. "I wouldn't say no to that; I don't think my ego could survive another one of your scowls. Bring those dimples on over."

Daisy burst into a fit of giggles as Tristan struck a pose and turned his head sideways to check his breath. "My lady would never forgive me."

"On the contrary, you owe him whatever kindness you can muster. You've been positively awful to him—and without cause. Do you admit it now?"

"With all my heart; I'm just so happy it's over and done with."

Then without thinking better of it, Daisy cupped Tristan's cheeks within her hands and pressed her lips to his, to the utter shock and astonishment of Tristan, who'd never meant for her to take the dare, and most certainly to Velena, who didn't know what to think at all. It lasted less than a second, but Daisy suddenly turned beat red as she pulled back, realizing what liberties she'd just taken.

"And you were worried about my behavior! Daisy, what on earth possessed you to…?"

"Come along Velena, I have plans for us this morning," Tristan interjected, absently wiping at his mouth with one hand, while pulling Velena out of the room with his other before she created a scene, however warranted it might be. "You do fine work—I…I mean you've been doing fine work in here so we'll be…be going now. Carry on, Daisy."

And with that they were out the door and into daylight before Velena could say another word. "Of all the nerve!" she began.

"Calm down."

"She deserves a keen beating."

"You practically gave her your blessing."

"I thought she'd kiss your cheek. It never occurred to me that she would…Tristan! Would you stop touching your mouth; you couldn't possibly have enjoyed that."

Tristan began to laugh as Velena tried harder to dig her way out of the hole of her own making.

"You laugh, but it's your fault too. What of Isulte? Shame on you! You weren't thinking of her at all."

"Me thinks the lady is jealous."

"You can *thinks* all you like, but that doesn't make it so. And stop laughing at me."

"All right. If it makes you feel any better, I'm just as embarrassed, and I'm sorry I dared her. Really, don't be angry with her. She's probably scared to death that you'll beat her or something."

"I may yet," she said, the start of a smile beginning to toy at the corners of her mouth.

"See there, it's funny. The whole thing deserves a good laugh if you stand back and look at it. It was just a kiss, after all."

"Just a kiss? I'm quite sure that was her first one, and look how she wasted it."

"I beg to differ!"

"I meant because she doesn't love you."

"Thank you for clarifying."

"And poor Bowan."

"Who's going to tell him?"

"You're right, of course, but I should be feeling sorry for you also, after she forced herself on you like that. I assume it was your first kiss as well."

"Then you would assume wrong."

Velena's mouth gaped open. "You've never mentioned it before."

"Some things are not worth mentioning."

Velena laughed as Tristan shook his head back and forth as if trying to rid himself of a bad memory.

"Tell me."

"It was none but our bailiff's saucy daughter. She took a liking to me, and had the intolerable habit of backing me into corners."

"As if you couldn't get away."

"I didn't always want to," he admitted sheepishly. "I realize how egregious this must sound to you—which is why I don't like talking about it."

Velena laughed. "Did she have fat ankles?"

"God help me if I looked! The truth was, and this makes it

worse, is that I hadn't any attraction for her whatsoever. I repented of it, if that counts for anything."

"I suppose it should. But no more kissing the help."

"I promise. The only think I want to get near my mouth is food. Let's see if the kitchen has anything they might hand out to two poor beggars."

"But supper's not for hours yet."

"I told my stomach that, but it doesn't believe me."

a poor match

As Tristan and Velena made their way into the great hall, they were forced to keep center or else chance being run down by the hubbub of activity going on in preparation for the coming evening.

Tables and benches were being rearranged, tapestries were being hauled outside to have the dust beaten out of them, and the old and dirty used up rushes were being replaced with new ones that did not contain the undesirable mixture of food debris, dog hair, cat feces, and spittle from those who chose not to do their spitting out of doors. Sweeping up the mess released such an unpleasant odor that Tristan and Velena felt compelled to cover their noses upon passing through from one end of the great hall to the other, where the dais was located.

Behind the large wooden dais was a curtain wall that hid a hallway leading to the kitchen, which was, itself, a wood framed add-on, built up against the right of the stone built hall. The actual cooking fires, deemed too much of a fire hazard to be a part of the kitchen, resided in yet another building off of that.

In charge of the kitchen and all its staff was Molly Fields, wife to the late Duncan Fields. She'd taken over her husband's job as head of the kitchen when he died of a foot infection five winters past. She was also, as she had been before her husband's death, the official ale taster, which made her the only individual in the village to make ale for the castle folk—for those within and those without.

She was forty years old now, but in good health. She had a thin wiry frame and was tall for a woman—even taller than most men, including her fifteen-year-old son who'd been a sickly child growing up. Roger Fields now worked alongside his mother as butler, which was to say, care taker of the ales.

Molly was busy at work kneading wastel dough when she looked up to see the couple walking in. "My goodness, Lord Tristan and Lady Velena, good morning to you! What can I do for you, Mistress?"

Tristan spoke up first, "The lady is anxious about our visitors today and would like something hot to drink to settle her nerves."

Velena turned to him laughing. "Don't use me as an excuse for your appetite."

"I have hot spiced wine we'll be using for tonight. But I've got so much of it, I'm sure two tumblers full won't be missed. Roger," she called out, "fetch the spiced wine from the buttery, my love. He's a good lad, always so helpful to his dear old mum."

She dusted her floury hands off on her apron and tucked several loose strands of sandy brown hair back up into her wimple[14] before retrieving two tumblers from a shelf.

"Well maybe you don't have a case of nerves, but no one would blame you if you did. I think we all have butterflies flying about in our stomachs today. Seems too short a time to get all things done up proper, but you need not think about that—we'll get it done. Seeing your cousin again is enough for you to think on, I'm sure." Molly continued, barely taking a breath in between sentences. "I've never seen him for myself, but I've heard tell he's quite handsome. If you don't mind my asking, is there any truth to that?"

Velena giggled, as much at the question as at Molly's personal enthusiasm of the subject. "He's very handsome, indeed. It'll be a poor match, I'm afraid."

"Pff," she sounded as she handed both cups to Roger who'd arrived to pour the wine. "Listen to her, Roger! Tell this humble noblewoman how beautiful she is."

"You're no doubt the prettiest lady I've ever seen," he replied awkwardly. "Though truthfully, I never seen no other fine lady before."

"Take the wine back now, Roger," Molly barked.

Velena smiled. "I'm not that humble; Peter is just that handsome."

"You just need to ask a gentleman. This fine esquire can tell you."

Velena turned to Tristan, expectantly, "Yes, esquire, what do you think of me?

"I've always thought you above average," he said, trying to hide a smile behind his cup.

Molly looked appalled. "Well you ought to be ashamed. Bred to be noble, but it doesn't ensure good manners."

"Did I ruin my chances of getting a slice of bread to go along with this heavenly drink?"

Molly pursed her lips. "And a slice of bread, he asks. Why not? I might as well get used to having extra food on hand with all our guests coming. A knight can eat his weight in armor! I wonder if that Squire Rowan will be among them. He's a charming devil, that one—and perhaps the only man taller than myself."

"How do you know who Rowan is, Molly?" Velena asked in surprise.

"He came once with Lord Magnus. They were passing through to somewhere or other, and had a whole passel of men with them. That was years ago, but when he was here, we had no more to eat after he left than those poor miserable creatures working the fiefs. He charmed me out of every slice of bread I had, not to mention minced pies. A bottomless pit, that one."

"As you said, he's tall. Perhaps, it all goes up. Last time I hugged him, I think my head came just shy of his shoulders."

Tristan feigned injury. "You never hug me."

"Jealous?"

"Please, over Rowan? He's only taller, handsomer, richer—wait a moment, maybe not richer. I think…"

Velena squinted her eyes. "Handsomer isn't a word."

"Yes, I think I'm richer—by far actually. I'm far, far...far, far richer."

"It's humility that's a virtue, Tristan, not pride. I think you're mixing them up."

"Oh, is that what I was doing?"

"Mmhm. But remind me again, did you ever spend time with Rowan aside from your stay at Landerhill?"

"I did. It was about the time he went from being Sir John's page to being his squire. Sir John was to escort Lord Magnus' wife, the Lady Madeline, to see one of her cousins in Oxfordshire, and Rowan accompanied him. Your aunt's cousin, just so happened to be a guest of my mothers. They all remained at our home three months, during which time Rowan ended up with very little to do. So whenever the both of us could get away, we'd spend our free time in town.

"Beggin' your pardon, my lady," Molly interrupted, "but could I get you anything else before I get my hands back into this dough?"

"No, Molly. We're quite satisfied," Velena said, handing over both their empty cups before taking their leave.

---

[14] **Wimple:** A head covering, made of cloth, worn around the neck and chin.

uncertainty

Although the day remained busy with last minute details, there was an anticipation that accompanied it, which made the work pleasant.

Tristan's solar received the addition of two extra chairs, as well as several other mattresses for the use of Lord Magnus' sons, and anticipated valets. The barracks were ready and so also the stalls, for both horses and any overflow of men.

Dinner had come and gone and the great hall was now being set up for supper, and for the arrival of their special guests. Velena had nothing more to do, and so she found herself wandering the bailey with Tristan trying to quiet her nerves. Tristan wanted only to soak up these last uninterrupted moments with Velena before everything had a chance to turn on its head.

They talked and laughed their way through the orchards and past the fish pond. They spent some time at the kitchen gardens also, but finally settled cross-legged in the grass beside the dog kennels. A female greyhound lay in between them, swollen with unborn puppies, happily accepting the attention Velena lavished upon the course gray fur of her neck.

"She looks so uncomfortable. Imagine carrying all those puppies inside you at one time."

"I'd rather not."

"I dare say, one at a time is trying enough for us humans."

"Again, I'm glad that can be narrowed down even further to just women."

Velena laughed, "I'm sure you are." Velena leaned back upon her hands. "I'm practically beside myself wondering if Jaren and Rowan are with Uncle Magnus." Velena turned her face heavenward and closed her eyes, "Oh, Lord, please let them be alive. I'm almost as excited to see them as I am to see Stuart."

"And not Peter?"

Velena looked sheepish. "I'm just nervous to see him. It was Stuart that Mother always brought me over to see. Uncle Magnus never got on well with Father, but he doted on his sister. He never spoke harshly to her, which I suppose was his way of being gentle. It was really their idea that Peter and I marry.

Velena grew quiet as a far off look passed over her face. Tristan waited for her to continue. "I wonder what sort of burial she received," she said picking at the grass around her skirt and tossing it aside. "Then again, what am I saying, Sir Tarek is an honorable man; I'm sure it was done properly. I felt certain, after she'd fallen ill, that we'd all come to ruin and that no one would be left to bury us. I used to be afraid that I'd be left to the dogs like those poor souls from the village." Silence.

"Those were awful days."

"You've come a long way."

"I suppose I have," she mused. "Everyone was so frightened, and none more than I. The girl that I was seems a stranger to me now. I'm thankful to God for pulling me out of that darkness—thankful to you too."

Tristan smiled at the compliment, "Any time, Velena...any time."

It was spoken casually, but Velena saw in his eyes that he was making her a promise. She wanted to expound on how much his help had meant to her, but he turned the conversation back to her uncle instead.

"Well, I'm sure it's safe to say that your uncle mourned his sister's passing, which would be a great compliment to your uncle, but out of curiosity, why does he not get along with your father?"

"Before arriving here I would have had no answer for you, but since our stay I've learned that Uncle Magnus disputed my parents' marriage after his own father died. He tried to have my mother married off to a wealthy count, which didn't work out, as the count wanted to be married to an even richer widow countess. Evidently, my father was the next best thing and he felt humiliated to come back to him."

"Ah, the mystery is solved."

"What mystery?"

"Of your uncle's cheery disposition."

"Oh, father's not really the reason for his disposition. In truth, Mother was the only one I ever saw him decent to. He's a harsh man. Hard on his sons, hard on his wife—ambitious."

"Most men are those things."

"Not you. You'd never lay a hand on your wife."

Tristan smirked, "I can't see myself doing it, but I'm not a husband yet either. I suppose if my wife speaks her mind to me as much as you do, she may have a couple of these coming her way," Tristan said, playfully pumping his fist in and out of his palm.

"Then I suppose I'd better brush up on my manners before Peter arrives, though I don't suppose there's enough time for that."

Tristan stopped his playing. "Velena, I wasn't being serious. I'm sure Peter would never have cause to hit you."

"One does not often escape the influences of their upbringing. So, I'm sure he will." They were both quiet.

"Does it frighten you?"

"It's not as if I've never known discipline before; I'm sure it'll be much the same."

Though abuse within a marriage was not uncommon, Tristan had never thought of it in relation to Velena before, and he found himself grieved and frustrated at his own inability to protect her from such a fate.

Velena threw grass at him, breaking his train of thought. "Stop looking so serious. It's what most women can expect from a marriage. I'm no different."

"If he touches you, I'll have to go from hating him in general to hating him specifically."

Velena frowned, "Don't hate him at all; I'll be alright. God is good, remember?"

Tristan took a deep breath. What would he give to protect this woman? It seemed that all was out of his control.

joy and sorrow

"I hope they get here soon. My stomach's growling so loud it'd wake the dead."

Velena, who's stomach was in absolute knots and couldn't even begin to fathom eating, ignored Daisy's distasteful remark and turned to face her. She smoothed back her hair for the hundredth time. "How's my hair, Daisy? My dress? Does it still give the impression you thought it would?"

"Aye, my lady. You need but only a little light to see that you're a lovely thing to behold."

"Thank you," Velena said as she let out a sigh and hugged the young woman before her. She released Daisy to follow the well-worn trail over to her window so that she could look out onto the black and white world below. "I'm so nervous. They should be here by now."

"Perhaps the dark overcame them and they had to make camp. It could be they won't arrive 'til morning at this rate. Hope that's not saying the same for our meal. Did I mention that I'm hungry?"

"More than once. Go see if the kitchen will take pity on you. I'm going to wait at the portcullis; I'm nearly crawling out of my skin for something to do."

Daisy nodded her head, smiling in understanding as she headed over to the desk to pick up two lit candles—one for Velena and one for herself.

Then, grabbing their cloaks, Daisy and Velena creaked their way down the stairs in silence, passing through the crowd of servants milling about before parting ways at the steps leading out of the keep.

Velena lifted her skirts above the muddy ground, and called over her shoulder for Daisy to let Tristan know where she was going if she ran across him. Having spent their day together, he'd sought some solitude to walk and pray. Velena felt for him and thought that she understood his concerns, but felt confident in her heart that he had nothing to fret about.

Anyone who knew anything about anything would be able to see what value there was in having a friend such as Tristan. She had inwardly determined to push that idea into Peter's mind, so that once the two of them became friends, there would be no issue with Tristan's visits and attentions, which would then be to them both as a couple. It would all work out in the end.

"Who goes there?" a masculine voice called out into the night. Sir Andret held his sword out in front of him, pointing it towards Velena.

Even in the dark she could discern a smile. "At least give me a chance to pick up a stick and defend myself."

"Nay, I trust you not, with a stick in your hands"

"Stop it," Velena said with a laugh. "Any sign of my uncle?"

"Not yet."

"Perhaps it's too dark."

Sir Andret shrugged his broad shoulders in answer. "The moon is full."

Velena smiled in agreement but took note that it was little more than a glow behind the blanket of clouds hanging overhead.

Then out of the trees it came, a muffled sound of wheels plodding over uneven earth and stone. Andret heard it first and looked toward Velena who was still studying the sky. "My lady."

"Yes." Velena looked over to see him holding his sword out towards the woods. A wagon! And men on horses! She could hear them now as they whinnied, instinct telling the tired animals that they were close to a warm barn and food aplenty.

Velena's heart beat faster, as she watched the distance close between them. She squinted her eyes, struggling to make out the first figures to trot their horses onto the bridge, when one of them jumped from his saddle and came running towards her.

"Velena!"

"Stuart? Stuart!" Velena held out her arms as her cousin swept her up into his strong embrace. She felt her feet leave the ground and thanked God for this little piece of Heaven on earth.

Stuart set her back onto the bridge, looking her over, his smile radiating his affection for her. "By Heaven it's good to see you—alive and well. You're beautiful, cousin."

Velena closed her eyes and smiled warmly, when two other figures approached her fast from behind. She heard their stampeding feet too late and let out a yelp as she felt herself being scooped up once again, but this time into the cradling arms of Rowan.

"Miss me?"

"Rowan." Velena barely breathed out his name before he tossed her to yet another pair of waiting arms, as if she weighed no more than a sack of grain. Cradled now by Jaren, Velena buried her face into her hands and wept. "Jaren. Oh, Rowan."

Jaren put her down and would have put his arms around her were it not for Rowan grabbing her to himself first."

"She said *my* name," Rowan grinned smugly, holding her close as she cried into his chest. "We're here, Velena." He chuckled, feeling the sting behind his own eyes. "Shhhh. Don't cry."

"You're alive. You're all alive!" Velena pulled back from Rowan's arms, looking back at the others.

"My heart's hurt for the years of not knowing; I don't have the words. I'm just happy. I'm just so very happy—and grateful to God for this moment."

They smiled in response, but exchanged looks that betrayed something yet to be told, causing Velena to peer out past them into the distance. The wagon was now rolling up onto the bridge at an even pace headed up by the thudding hooves of her uncle on horseback, his bulky silhouette giving him away. The absence of a certain someone riding beside him sounded like a battle cry in Velena's heart.

Velena worked to wipe the tears from her eyes. "Where's Peter?" she whispered, not wanting to ask the question aloud.

Stuart approached her, his blue eyes indiscernible in the dark. "He's not here. He's gone, Velena. Peter and our mother, both."

Velena felt as though the wind had been squeezed from her lungs. It took her a moment to find her voice and then all she could say was, "Oh."

The happiness that had first spurred her to tears was replaced with sorrow—and her tears now trailed, unchecked, down her face and throat, watering the neckline of her tunic. "I was rather hoping that he just didn't want me anymore. At least then he'd still be alive. I'm sorry for your loss." Velena covered her mouth as a sob escaped with her last word spoken.

Stuart held her close. "I'm sorry for yours. I know you expected us to deliver you a husband, not a bunch of idiot men."

Velena smiled through her tears. "I like men," she said, causing them all to laugh, despite the pity they still carried in their eyes. Velena was glad when Sir Andret interrupted.

"Jaren."

The squire turned to face him. "Andret! Thank God!" The brothers came together in a hearty embrace, glancing back towards the group only once before disappearing through the portcullis, both men wiping their eyes, too moved to speak.

As they passed into shadow, Rowan noticed Tristan leaning up against the stony archway. He'd waited to make himself known, wanting Velena to have her moment. He'd been hoping, for her sake, that Peter had been among the group, but if he was honest with himself, he was relieved that he wasn't, and found himself praying to be forgiven for his selfishness.

"What, are you too good for us? Where's my hug?" Rowan called into the dark.

"I was going to jump into your arms, but Velena got there first."

"Well, come on over, it's not too late," Rowan said with a laugh, meeting Tristan halfway. It seemed that no one could get too much of one another, as embraces were followed up with back slaps, and firm handshakes—as if letting go would mean losing them all over again.

Lord Magnus came up beside Velena and his son, as the wagon rolled by. He didn't dismount. "Hello, Niece."

"Hello, Uncle." Velena looked up at him, unable to see his face clearly from below. "I'm sorry for your loss. I wonder that you didn't send word of it."

Magnus spurred his horse on and continued after the wagon at a walk. "I had my reasons."

"Yes, Uncle," Velena said as she hurried her pace to match that of the horse.

From atop his saddle, Magnus looked down at his niece. The moon lit her upturned face as she spoke, and outlined her figure as she struggled to keep up. "You've grown into a beautiful woman, Velena. Peter would have been proud to have such a fine looking wife."

"Thank you Uncle."

"Where's your father?"

"In the great hall. Supper's waiting for you."

Magnus snorted his disapproval. "He couldn't greet his brother-in-law at the door. I have to go in and search him out, is that it? This is fine hospitality?"

"Father." Stuart spoke up from Velena's side, leading his own horse by the reigns.

"Don't *Father* me. Your uncle slights us."

"I'm sure it's my fault," Velena interjected. "I caused such a scene greeting everyone that I'm sure I was a distraction from word being sent that you'd arrived. Of course he would've met you at the gate if he'd known."

"No one's blaming you, girl. You've got enough servants standing around gawking at us like we've each arrived with three heads; nothing is stopping them now. Go on and let your master know we've arrived," he barked, causing men to scatter and run ahead of them.

"Allow them to tend to your horses, as well, and come with me, Uncle—all of you. We have so much to talk about. There's a fire and food all waiting inside."

"Did someone say food?" Rowan spoke up from somewhere behind them.

Tristan walked next to Rowan observing Velena's uncertain behavior—decidedly frustrated with the effect her uncle was having over her. Then came his next thought. Peter was dead. What would this mean for her? What would it mean for them? He wondered when she would get the chance to digest the fact that there would be no marriage. He didn't know when he'd have a moment to speak with her, but it was his chief priority.

But he wasn't to receive any answers this night, for the evening went long, as candles and torches burnt bright, adding their light to the fire places that were kept blazing in their hearths.

Knights lifted their glasses and toasted Wineford's newest arrivals, everyone eating their fill, and then some—grateful for a warm room and a full belly.

a truth revealed

The following morning Velena awoke to a semi-lit room. She raised herself up on her elbows, and looked toward her shuttered window, as the first rays of morning began to penetrate through the cracks, illuminating her surroundings in a soft and peaceful glow. She fell back against her pillow and rubbed the sleep from her eyes.

Peter was dead. This was her first thought. The Plague had taken him from her. No, not the plague—it was God. But this fact didn't hold the despair that it had when her mother was taken. Velena clung to the truth this time, and the truth was now firmly planted in her heart. *God is good,* she repeated to herself, and *His ways are not my ways.*

She didn't really mourn the cousin that she barely knew, but she did mourn the husband that she hoped to have had. She leaned over to peer at Daisy, who continued to sleep soundly on the trundle below, smiling at the bedfellow that would continue to be hers. She knew that God had other plans for her, other than marrying Peter. This was now obvious, but what were they?

She wanted to talk with Tristan. She hadn't had the opportunity to speak with him in the great hall the night before, not that she'd even thought of it. Naturally, she'd been very distracted. Her uncle had been busy giving everyone detailed accounts of the devastation left by the Plague.

Left to ruin, he'd said. In many villages, abandoned homes were caving in, animals having run off or died. Magnus swore that the skeletons lay so still and quiet, that he felt certain not even the spirits of the dead dared to linger about anymore.

He'd spoken of people coming over from Holland, calling themselves Flagellants, who had taken to roaming the countryside. Barefoot and half-naked, they whipped themselves with nail-bearing scourges, preaching the importance of penance, by way of self-mutilation, as being the only way to gain the attention and mercy of God. When they'd first entered Landerhill Township, all but one had lain themselves out upon the ground in the form of a cross. The man still standing then took up the leather straps and whipped the others with them, eventually exchanging places with one of his fellow flagellants, so that he also might receive his share of the abuse.

Reportedly, London had seen hundreds of these Flagellants perform such rituals, but fortunately, in Totness, it was only a meager group of ten men that had trickled in. It was Peter and Stuart who'd finally chased them away. One good thing was that the gruesome event had happened over a year ago, as did the most devastating effects to their town. Her uncle seemed convinced that the Plague had now run its course, and so was seeking to bring her family back with him.

Velena shuddered beneath her covers, thankful she hadn't dreamed of any of it. She decided not to go back to sleep.

Gently, she climbed out over Daisy, causing only a slight stir and twitch in her eye. She dressed quietly, struggling with her cuffs, before haphazardly plaiting her long dark locks of unruly hair, which she then tossed over her shoulder. She grabbed her cloak and shoes and padded silently out through the door.

Downstairs, she gingerly tiptoed around valets, nobles, and servants alike until she reached Tristan, who had traded his comfortable feather bed for a straw mat against the far end of the wall by the bookcase. Glancing around to see who might be looking, she kicked him in the foot until his eyes began to flutter open.

"Wha—?"

"Shhh." Velena motioned with her head for him to follow her to the door.

Initial irritation that she would wake him up so early, was soon replaced with a feeling of concern that something might be wrong. He watched her exit the room, and quickly got up to join her outside. Sucking in his breath as his stockinged feet hit the frigid stone steps, he shut the door gently behind him expecting some tears, or at the very least a conversation centered around Peter's death, but was taken aback when faced only with an impish grin.

"Let's bring Rowan and Jaren breakfast in bed."

"Breakfast in b—in the stables? Kings eat breakfast, and I'm sure they're just happy to be warm."

"Just some bread and wine. You know how much Rowan loves to eat. I want to see them. I can't stand that they're here after all this time and they're still asleep."

"There's a reason for that. It was a long trip and they already had their fill of wine last night. It's too early for me as well; I think you ought to go this one alone."

"I need a chaperon."

"I'm not sure that I qualify."

"Why is that?"

"*I'm a man,*" he stated with emphasis.

"Nooo, you're *my Tristan.*"

He rolled his eyes, "I'm your Tristan? Thank you for that lovely sentiment, but get Daisy, so *your Tristan* can go back to sleep."

"You're already friends with Rowan; I want you to come."

"Should I put on a skirt first?"

"Don't be silly."

"*I'm* the silly one? Pff! One of us is being very silly, but it isn't me. Goodnight."

"It's morning, and I'll be waiting at the kitchen; go get your cloak."

"I won't come."

"I'll still wait," Velena cooed, backing down the stairs, fashioning her mouth into the perfect pout, "...cold, forlorn, abandoned."

"Fine, I'll get my shoes."

Velena clapped her hands together and ran for the kitchen.

Tristan arrived moments later to find her armed with a basket and a smile.

"Since you have me up and coherent, I wanted to ask you how you're fairing with the news of your cousin," he said, gesturing for her to lead the way.

Velena's smile wavered as she moved forward and set the pace. "I find myself thinking about that passage you once shared with me from Deuteronomy. Do you remember?"

"About God bringing the Israelites out of Egypt?"

"Yes. With His *mighty hand* and *outstretched arm*, He was merciful to them. He heard them. At the time you shared that with me, I didn't believe it. I didn't believe that He really saw our afflictions…or that He cared for me.

"I remember," Tristan said, cocking his head sideways to study her face, properly.

Velena smiled. "I do, now. And the rest of it says that He brought them to a place of milk and honey. This place has been that for me. It was here that He called me to Himself. He used you as a light that would lead me out of that horrible place of darkness. He brought me here! *His mighty outstretched arm* brought *me* to a place of safety, and—and I'm so humbled by that!"

Velena's eyes grew glassy. "So even though Peter is gone, I've already seen the Lord's goodness for myself. So, I know that I can trust Him for my future. Whatever it may be."

Tristan inhaled deeply. "If we could only ever remember that."

"What, exactly?"

"That we all live and breathe beneath the outstretched arms of a merciful God. What concerns would we ever have worth speaking of, if we could remember that?"

Velena looked out at the uncertain future set before her—and smiled. "I dare say, none."

Both thoughtful now, they kept up a brisk walk as they traversed the remaining distance to the stables. The air was chilly and the birds were just beginning to greet the world around them. The wooden door creaked and the horses raised their heads in curiosity as the pair entered the warmth that so much horseflesh provided.

Velena lead the way to the empty stalls toward the back and then stood still, staring down at a sleeping Rowan. Though two-and-a-half years had done a lot to mature his boyishly pleasing features into that of a mature twenty-year-old man, he was still much the same as she remembered. He had a smallish nose and a large mouth that happened to complement one another well, along with blue eyes, and hair that was so blond that it was almost white.

She could see that he'd grown his hair out much longer then was considered to be masculine, but it didn't surprise her that he'd do something out of the normal, just to spite everyone else. He had it pulled back and knotted up towards the crown of his head, and though having never seen one up close, herself, she imagined he bore a strong resemblance to an albino Scott.

Jaren, on the other hand, though tall, was only tall enough to outsize his two older brothers, but came nowhere near the size of Rowan. He had brown eyes, thick bushy eyebrows, and medium brown hair worn at the acceptable length of just below his earlobes. Only he wasn't in the barn to be observed just then.

"Where's Jaren?" Velena whispered.

Tristan shrugged.

"It's like I'm dreaming—seeing everyone again. Up till now, it's felt like we've been on an island. He's sleeping so sweetly."

"He's not a puppy."

Velena giggled. "I feel badly about waking him up now."

"Well, if I got up for nothing, then I'm going back to sleep."

Startled, Velena watched as Tristan hunkered down, crawling beneath the empty blankets Jaren had left beside Rowan.

"So you leave me out here in the cold do you?" she hissed.

Rowan suddenly stirred, wordlessly pulling back his blankets. His eyes were still closed but he provided her with an inviting grin.

Velena rushed in between them, flopping down on her stomach

and turning her head to face the squire.

Rowan gave her a lazy smile and spoke in a gravelly voice. "I can see that years of seclusion have all but thrown out your sense of decorum."

"I wanted to see you. Where's Jaren?" she asked, her voice sweet and light.

"Who cares? You make a much better bed fellow."

"I won't tell him you said so."

"I'll have to brag about it, myself, then. I've never slept beside a woman before, so this is a treat."

Tristan cleared his throat to object.

Rowan smiled. "I said *slept.*"

"We're not sleeping," Velena corrected.

"What are we doing then?"

"Cuddling for warmth."

"Cuddling?" Rowan seemed to wake up, his eyes now full of mischief. "I don't think I've ever cuddled with a woman before either. I'm not sure this is how it goes. I don't know about you, Tristan, but I feel wholly inadequate to the task. Is this how you would describe such an event?"

Tristan played along. "I'm not really sure. I mean I've imagined cuddling up to a woman. I guess I'd have to ask one if I'm to know how to do it properly. Oh look, here's one now."

"Well, speak of the devil, would you teach us how to cuddle, Velena?"

Velena rolled her eyes. "No."

"Oh come on, what's a little bonding between friends," Rowan reasoned inching his way closer until she felt herself squeezed in between the two. He reached his arm across her back, over top of the blankets.

Velena buried her face in her hands, protesting in muffled tones. "I take all my nice words back. I forgot how horrible you were; and almost three years absent has made you worse."

Rowan laughed and carried on as if her words gave him all the more incentive to continue. "Is this how it's done Velena?" A leg now flopped over her ankles.

Tristan followed suit from the other side. "Are we cuddling now?"

"Stop it, the pair of you! Get off me or you're not getting any breakfast!"

"Breakfast? Why didn't you say so," Rowan said, releasing her. He sat up rubbing his hands together, exposing a well-muscled bare chest.

Velena would have blushed except she was still pinned face down by Tristan's leg flopped atop hers. "Tristan you're still there."

"I'm not hungry—I'd rather cuddle."

Velena threw his limb off as she raised herself up on all fours and wiggled out from beneath the blankets, coming to stand above them. "I can see my kind acts are only taken advantage of. Rowan, you are a negative influence on Tristan. Tristan, you are easily swayed. I'll be leaving now."

"Come back," Tristan called after her.

"No."

"Come on. I'm *your Tristan*, remember? Remember that?"

"Not anymore," she said stomping her way out through the doors, causing great guffaws and chuckles to follow in her wake.

Rowan placed a hand to his naked midsection and let out a long satisfied sigh. "Making her mad never gets old."

"I've found, that on occasion, it really does."

Rowan snickered in between bites of soft wastel. "Have some," he said with his mouth still full. He broke off a piece from the loaf and tossed it to Tristan. "It's fantastic!"

"Thanks," he said catching it one handed.

"That's right, so you've been stuck up here with her for the past few years."

"Something like that." Tristan smiled but didn't elaborate.

Rowan studied him over his jug of wine.

"You'd be hoping falsely if you're thinking Peter's death will be in your favor where she's concerned."

"No, no—nothing like that."

"I'm not sure I believe you."

Tristan shrugged as he accepted a drink from Rowan, wiping his mouth with the back of his hand. "Believe what you like."

Unaffected, Rowan continued stuffing his mouth full of bread. "Fair enough."

It was a man's conversation. No mincing of words, simply mutual disagreement and acceptance—comradery at its finest. The gulf of time had closed between Rowan and Tristan with few words spoken and Tristan found himself very satisfied in his company. After all, it had been almost three years since he'd had a male companion with which to sit and talk with—or not talk with, which was equally as fine a thing. Velena had many fine qualities, but not talking was not one of them.

Meal finished, they both got up and stepped outside, Rowan grabbing his blue and green tunic on the way out. The scent of dew was strong in the air, and he inhaled of it deeply, overjoyed to be away from the stench of town. Rowan stretched his arms out wide and let out a yelp, air vapor rising to the sky. "Glory! This is a fine English day."

Tristan leaned up against the hitching post and stared back towards the keep. "What's the real reason Lord Magnus didn't write about Peter?"

"He knows the Baron can't stand him, and that with his sister dead, he might not have been welcomed so readily if Lord Richard had known he was coming empty handed, as it were."

"Why did he come then? He all but said the Plague was gone."

"Stuart."

"Ah," Tristan said, realizing now that he intended to fill one brother's spot with the other. "Does he love her?"

Rowan gave Tristan an incredulous look just before disappearing through the neck hole of his tunic. "Why should that matter to *you?*"

Tristan began to tap his middle finger against the rail he was resting against. "I just think she ought to be loved."

"Ought we all, but that's a luxury not many of us get, my friend. But if it sets your mind at ease, yes, he wants her. Peter didn't, so she'll be getting the better end of the stick."

"You don't speak well of him?"

"Peter was an ass." Rowan cleared his throat and expectorated, as if to add weight to his point.

"Like father like son, is that it?"

"There's an understatement. Velena's uncle is no picnic, but at least you know what you're getting. Peter, on the other hand, knew how to put on a good face. There was no trusting him."

Something squeezed at Tristan's heart knowing what would have awaited her in Peter, and he thanked God for saving her from such a fate. He knew as well as anyone that love played very little role in the start of most marriages, but if there was ever a person who deserved such affection, it was Velena.

"And Stuart?"

"Less of an ass. You'll get a different answer from Jaren, of course, but to think that Magnus could turn out a son of shining white character would be to not think at all."

Rowan disappeared back into the stables and came out hopping on one foot as he pulled on his second shoe. He looked up to see Jaren and Sir Andret approaching in the distance. Sir Andret carried a falcon upon his arm and Jaren, the bird's kill. "By Heaven, he's got a falcon! I've got to get a closer look at him." And with that he strode off in their direction.

Tristan walked after him, inwardly hoping that Rowan was being overly critical of Stuart and that Jaren's higher opinion of him would prove true.

profession of love

Velena had been on an irritated, but direct, path back to the keep when she bumped into a very delighted Stuart on his way out. She rewarded him with a brilliant smile, quickly holding out her hands for him to take.

He raised them to his lips. "I thought you were still in bed."

"I got up early."

"I'm glad for it; do you have somewhere to be or might I steal you away for a walk."

"Certainly," she answered, clasping her hands behind her back while pivoting herself away from the steps. "Would you care for a walk around the fish pond or the orchards?"

"Where is your favorite place to walk?"

Velena instantly thought of the stream in the woods, but answered the orchard instead.

They walked side by side, glancing at each other from time to time, slightly awkward in each other's company.

"You look different," Velena finally spoke.

"So do you."

"Do you approve?"

"I'm still trying not to stare."

Velena smiled, shyly.

"How about me?" he asked.

"You look…"

"Stronger."

"I was going to say..."

"More handsome?"

Velena laughed. "Confident."

"Confident?" Stuart smiled to himself, "Yes, I could agree with that. I know what I want."

"What's that?"

He looked over at her, enjoying the way her hips swayed when she held her hands behind her back that way.

"In good time, cousin."

"A secret?"

"Good timing," he clarified.

Velena's curiosity was aroused, but she felt confident she'd wheedle it out of him before their walk was over.

"Do you remember my governess?"

"Yes," Velena said recalling the memory of the sour faced woman. "We were most likely the bane of her existence."

"Well said. We could always find the best places to hide from her, and she never did tell our parents how rotten we'd been for fear that Father would punish her for losing us in the first place."

"Poor woman; she was forever running after us with that twisted up look on her face."

"That's what you called her, remember?"

"What?"

"Miss Twist."

"I never did!" Velena protested.

"Yes—yes you did. I remember it distinctly."

Velena laughed and raised her eyes skyward as if trying to recover a long lost memory. "I suppose I must have—though I have a difficult time thinking that I could ever have been so disrespectful."

"Not you."

"No, I should say not."

"Ha! You say a lot more things than not. How are you still so respected among you peers?"

"I've only had one to contend with, as of late. But why, sir, did you bring up dear Miss Twist?"

Stuart was still deciding if she was referring to that messy haired esquire he'd seen in the hall, but answered as though he wasn't the least bit curious. "Ah yes, as I was saying, we were wonderful at hiding, but she wasn't so terrible at seeking, if I recall. She'd always find us just before she had to answer to my father for our whereabouts. Except the once."

Velena held up her finger and then pointed it down. "Under the bed in the guest bedroom!"

"Yes, under the *bed.*"

Something about the way Stuart said *bed* changed the aura of the conversation, though Velena couldn't have pin pointed how.

They'd reached the orchards and were now in the midst of them when he stopped walking and turned to face her. "What were you, seven? Eight? I remember looking over at you, your hair in a tangled mess…"

Velena giggled.

"You couldn't stop smiling. I can still remember you, pressing your fingers against your lips signaling me to be silent as Miss Twist paced back and forth through the halls." Stuart reached his hand out to tug at a loose strand of hair that had made its way out of its plait. "How I hated the day you began to wear your hair back."

"Stuart?"

"I knew I loved you then."

Velena's skin began to tingle in response to his touch and some sort of hot and cold sensation was coursing its way up to her head making her feel faint. "You knew no such thing. You were ten."

"You don't think a boy of ten knows about love?"

"It's unlikely."

"What about a man of twenty?"

Velena had to look down, feeling self-conscious under so intense a gaze. "Not many men have the privilege of loving whom they wish."

"I do."

Her eyes rose to meet his. "You are the second man to tell me so, and I can't help but feel envious of this choice, when my own is limited to loving only whom my father chooses for me—though Tristan would tell me that this is not a poor place to be. For those who have a choice are limited by the number of those who do as well, and of those there are few, who are not promised to someone else." Velena knew she was rambling, but she didn't know what else to say.

Stuart could have added that he was not, indeed, free to love whomever he wished, but instead just happened to love she whom his father had chosen for him—but he held his tongue. This was the second time Velena had referred to this Tristan, and his curiosity was quickly getting the better of him.

"Who is it again that's been staying here with you?

"Tristan Challener. You know him."

Stuart looked doubtful.

"At least when we were children you did. You were about twelve, I think. I was ten. Lord Rolland brought him along on one of his visits to Landerhill for Hocktide. All the adults would bet on our cockfights. Don't you remember?"

"Was he there?"

"Stuart, really. His bird always won; I think you could remember something about it. I recall Jaren being so angry, that he convinced the rest of us not to speak two words to Tristan the rest of the week."

"Perhaps that's why I have only a vague inclination of him. When Jaren gave an order I listened."

"The tables have turned have they not? It seemed to me, last night, that he now takes his cues from you."

Stuart shrugged. "We were both squiring under Sir John, along with Rowan, when the Plague took him and six others from the barracks in one night. We were left to ourselves for a while, floundering in our training."

"The whole world seemed to stop, did it not?" Velena said, riveted by the account.

"It did. But I was unwilling to die before I was actually dead. I continued my training, and pushed Jaren to do the same, reminding him that his brothers, Sir Andret and Sir Makaias, may yet be living, and so he had a reason to stay strong."

"What was your reason?"

"Are you so unperceptive?"

There was that tingle again. "But Peter..."

"*Was* the luckiest man alive...and now I have the chance to be."

definitions

Definitions are in the order they appear in *Beneath Outstretched Arms*.

[1] **Villeins:** A feudal tenant.

[2] **Solar:** A bedroom and living space.

[3] **Demesne:** Land attached to a manor, and retained for the owner's own use.

[4] **Pillory:** A punishment device, fashioned with holes for securing both the head and the hands. Most often used as a means of public humiliation.

[5] **Quintain:** An object or dummy, mounted on the moveable cross bar of a post, used as a target for the lance.

[6] **Portcullis:** A heavy latticed grille, vertically-closing gate.

[7] **Dais:** A raised platform used for a speaker, seats of honor, or a throne.

[8] **Plait:** A braid (pronounced "plat").

[9] **Yeomen:** A commoner, cultivating a small land estate; a freeholder.

[10] **Wardrober:** Servant in charge of his master's clothing.

[11] **Garderobe:** A small chamber where the toilet is located.

[12] **Embrasure:** The opening between the two upright solid portions (merlons) of a battlement.

[13] **Merlon:** The solid upright portion of a battlement.

[14] **Wimple:** A head covering, made of cloth, worn around the neck and chin.

acknowledgements

The idea for this series was born in the winter of 2006, when I had only one child and a night job at a department store putting up those little yellow price papers that are now, conveniently, digital. My first thoughts were penned on the backs of these, and they are now safely tucked away as nostalgic memorabilia.

Over the next nine years, I kept my story on the back burner. The thought of doing all of the research needed for a medieval novel, while trying to homeschool our four children, seemed absolutely daunting. So deciding that it just wasn't the right season in life to give myself over to personal projects, I carried around a story inside of me, that would occasionally find its way out by way of random chapters, that I could visualize so clearly, that I just had to be put them down on paper. As always, I would tuck them away for "someday."

Then on one not so apparently amazing day, in 2015, after reading through the *Trade Winds* trilogy by Linda Chaikin, the Lord said, *okay—it's time*. That was all I needed to hear! From that moment on, I was on a mission, bringing home armloads of research material from the library and searching high and low for every scrap of paper I had ever written a chapter, phrase, or sentence upon. I printed off the computer every file that I could find that I'd saved for "someday." I laid them all out on the floor and began putting the lives of Tristan and Velena in order. There were gaps to be filled, plot points to be changed, and chapters that needed to be written and rewritten, but I had enough for my back burner dream to become a trilogy—and now, consequently, a novel series of four.

Thank you, Heavenly Father, for allowing me the opportunity, through this book, to thank You for just a few of Your infinite gifts to me.

Thank you to my husband, Aaron. You are my dream catcher. You have patiently listened (and fallen asleep) to countless renditions of the same chapters, over and over again; offering your opinions, constructive criticisms, and in some cases, telling me in no uncertain terms, that "a man wouldn't do that," whenever I strayed too close to the feminine. You were the first person to laugh out loud at my written attempts at humor, and the first person I want to thank for being a part of my story. I love you.

Thank you to my children, Aloria, Justus, Selia and little Vienna. You have all been so understanding as to why mommy gets to be on her computer all the time when you, yourselves, have time limits. God bless your little hearts!

Thank you, Mom and Dad, for all of your support—and Mom, for reading through my book at least four plus times, and for loving it each and every one of them.

Thank you to everyone at Selah Press for walking with me through this new and exciting process. To you especially, Kayla, for your ongoing friendship. My relationship with your family has been one of the joys of my life! Thank you Loral for your meticulous editing of this book, and for allowing me my voice. Thank you Jennifer for all of the work you put into my cover design.

Thank you Amy, for the stunning cover art! Your approaching me to do it, was one of the biggest blessings of this whole project, and confirmation to me that the Lord was in this. You gave a face to Velena, and I am forever grateful.

Thank you, Alisa, for extending to me your creative talents last minute for my scripture page. Your beautifully designed scripture coloring calendars have offered me many moments of precious peace and relaxation. Grown up coloring is one of life's greatest inventions, and just looking at them brightens my day. (Discover them for yourself at etsy.com/shop/AlisaTaylorDesign)

Thank you Sarah and Leah, my dear sweet Christian sisters, for sharing in my joys. Thank you, Sarah, for asking to read through my book, despite your hectic family schedule. You have always been a faithful friend, and I treasure you. Thank you, Leah, for so readily making yourself available via computer and phone, to read through my chapters, to discuss important plot line decisions, and to talk me out of killing off important characters that needed to stick around. Your listening ear and honest advice have been invaluable to making this book what it is. Geography holds no bearing over our hearts; we are kindred spirits, no matter the distance between us.

And last, but certainly not least, thank you, Justin and Jaqueline—thank you for your friendship, your loyalty, and your lasting influence on my life. Justin, without you, there would be no Tristan.

Follow Venessa Knizley to receive news on the release of book 2 of the *Walk With Me* series, an opportunity to preorder, and chances to win a free ebook.

Facebook: Facebook.com/venessaknizley
Twitter: @nessipher

Made in the USA
Lexington, KY
25 April 2016